LOVE TIMES TWO

Cassie wrote in her diary for a long time, describing the evening in detail. Whenever she came to T.J.'s name, she drew a little heart around it, knowing it was silly but taking pleasure in it just the same. When she had finished, she reread what she'd written, smiling to herself, then added a few more sentences.

"I was kidding when I wrote before that I was falling madly in love with T.J., but now I think I really am. I asked Claudia if she thought he was beginning to feel the same way, and she told me to ask him. Fat chance!" Suddenly Cassie's eyes widened as a new thought struck her. She wrote the final sentence very slowly: "I wonder if she's falling in love with him herself."

She closed the diary and looked over at her twin, who was staring out the half-opened balcony door at the moon-drenched sky. *Oh, why couldn't she fall in love with Don instead?* thought Cassie. *Or why couldn't I?*

Bantam Sweet Dreams Romances
Ask your bookseller for the books you have missed

Love Times Two

Stephanie Foster

BANTAM BOOKS
TORONTO • NEW YORK • LONDON • SYDNEY • AUCKLAND

RL 6, IL age 11 and up

LOVE TIMES TWO
A Bantam Book / July 1984

Cover photo by Pat Hill

ISBN 0-553-24153-2

Published simultaneously in the United States and Canada

Bantam Books are published by Bantam Books, Inc. Its trademark, consisting of the words ''Bantam Books'' and the portrayal of a rooster, is Registered in U.S. Patent and Trademark Office and in other countries. Marca Registrada. Bantam Books, Inc., 666 Fifth Avenue, New York, New York 10103.

PRINTED IN THE UNITED STATES OF AMERICA

O   0 9 8 7 6 5 4 3 2 1

For Joanna and Louise, my twinspirations

Chapter One

When Cassie Fletcher first opened her eyes, it took her a few drowsy moments to realize where she was. She squinted up at the knotty pine ceiling a few feet above her head, then at the early morning sunshine filtering through the yellow and white curtains at the window. The air smelled of pine and freshly brewed coffee. She could hear the gentle lapping of water nearby. Of course—Green Lake! The Fletchers had arrived late the night before, and both Cassie and Claudia, her twin, had been dazed with sleep and cramped after the long drive from southern Pennsylvania to upstate New York.

The girls had helped their parents unload the car and taken a quick look around the cabin the family had rented from their friends the Fergusons for the month of July. They'd gone out on the dock to admire the silent, moonlit lake, then dragged their suitcases and themselves up the stairs to their little bedroom. Cassie had opted for the upper bunk and Claudia the lower. Now, as Cassie lay in the top bunk, she wondered if her sister was awake.

"Claude?" Cassie called, hanging her head over the side of her bed to peer at the lower bunk. It was empty. Then she became aware of a shadow moving rhythmically against the curtains. Cassie swung down to the floor without using the ladder and padded to the door that led to a small balcony overlooking the lake. When she opened it, she was dazzled for a moment by the sunlight dancing on the water. Then she saw her sister, clad in a turquoise bikini, using the balcony railing as a barre while she performed her morning warm-up exercises. Claudia was very serious about modern dance and never, even on vacation, neglected her warm-ups.

"Hi, sleepyhead," said Claudia, glancing over her shoulder as she bent and stretched, her long blond ponytail swinging as she moved.

"Why didn't you wake me?" Cassie asked, brushing her hair, almost the same shade as Claudia's but short and tousled, out of her eyes.

Claudia grinned at her, braces flashing. "You were snoring so peacefully, I couldn't bear to disturb you." She extended one slender leg, resting her heel on the railing, and bent gracefully at the waist, touching her bare toes with the opposite hand.

"I do not snore!" objected Cassie, doing a few deep-knee bends and wincing as her complaining muscles reminded her of the previous day's drive. If she could find some tennis courts around, she'd be able to work out that stiffness in half a set.

"OK, you don't snore, but you sure make some weird noises when you sleep," her twin teased. Having completed her exercises, Claudia leaned her elbows on the railing and took a deep breath of the fresh, pine-scented air. "Isn't this positively the most beautiful place in the world?" she said with a sigh.

Leaning beside her, Cassie had to agree that it was. The lake stretched before them, sparkling with a million pinpoints of reflected sunlight and rimmed with tall, dark trees. On the opposite shore stood a few old wooden docks, and the outline of a house or two could be seen farther back in the woods. To the girls' right, a small wooded island rose out of the water like an illustration from a child's picture book, romantic and somehow mysterious.

"Hello, up there!" called a voice from below. Claudia and Cassie looked down to see their mother on the deck, a tray laden with a coffee-pot and four mugs in her hands. She was wearing her new striped bathing suit and looked, Cassie thought, much too young to be the mother of two sixteen-year-old daughters. "The coffee's made, and I'm about to put on the bacon. Come on down. There's time for a quick swim before breakfast."

"Where's Daddy?" asked Claudia.

"He's checking out the boathouse. There's a rowboat, I think, and some fishing poles. He'll be here in a minute." Mrs. Fletcher set the tray on a picnic table and began pouring coffee as the twins turned to go inside. Suddenly Claudia paused and shaded her eyes, looking out over the water.

"Who do you think that could be?" she asked Cassie.

"What are you looking at?" her sister responded.

4

"There's a canoe coming across the lake, and it's headed straight for our dock."

Cassie now saw the canoe, too, tiny as a toy, gliding across the water. She realized that she was still in her pajamas and scooted inside to change. Whoever it was, she wasn't about to be spotted in her pj's.

A few minutes later, the girls came down-stairs, Cassie now clad in a bright red tank suit, her short honey blond hair brushed to a shine. Their mother had just started the bacon, and they carried bread, jam, and fruit out to the deck, where Mr. Fletcher, in bathing trunks and a T-shirt, was examining a somewhat cracked and weathered oar.

Claudia and Cassie helped themselves to coffee. "Is there another one?" Cassie asked her father, indicating the oar.

"There are three, none of them the same size," Mr. Fletcher told her. "This one's in pretty bad shape, but I can probably fix it. I think I have some duct tape in the trunk of the car."

"Oh, Daddy," said Claudia affectionately, "you think you can fix anything with duct tape! I bet if one of us broke a leg, you'd wrap it up with duct tape!"

Mr. Fletcher shrugged. "And why not? It's

5

probably the same stuff doctors use, only they call it something else."

"Hey, gang, I think we have a visitor," said Mrs. Fletcher, looking out over the water. "I'd better get another cup. And I'll turn that bacon, or else we'll have charcoal and eggs for breakfast."

She went back into the cabin as the girls and their father watched the approach of the canoe with interest. A young man paddled the craft expertly, the muscles of his strong, suntanned arms working rhythmically. Sunlight glinted off his wavy brown hair. He wore cut-off jeans and a sleeveless orange T-shirt. A pair of beat-up sneakers rested on the seat in the canoe's prow. Cassie guessed he was about seventeen. She glanced at Claudia. Wordlessly, they communicated: *Wow! Definitely good-looking.*

Mr. Fletcher stood up and leaned over the deck railing as the canoe glided to a silent stop by the dock. "Good morning!" he called. "Ahoy, or avast, or something."

The boy looked up, and Claudia and Cassie caught a glimpse of the warmest, richest brown eyes either of them had ever seen. "Hi. I'm T.J. Howard," the boy said, mooring the canoe and climbing onto the dock. "Welcome to Green Lake. You're the Fletchers, right?"

"Right," said Mr. Fletcher, going down the rickety wooden steps to the dock and extending his hand. "I'm Frank Fletcher, and these are my twin daughters, Claudia and Cassie." Cassie sucked in her stomach and beamed. Claudia, she noticed, had formed her mouth into a tight-lipped smile, as she always did upon meeting someone who didn't know she wore braces. Her Mona Lisa look, Cassie called it.

"Twins? You don't look alike," T.J. noted.

"We're fraternal twins, not identical," Cassie said.

Mrs. Fletcher reappeared at that moment and said, "Hi, I'm Lydia Fletcher. Would you like a cup of coffee? We were just about to have breakfast. Please join us."

"No, thanks," said T.J. "I already ate. My mom and dad asked me to stop by on my way to the store to say hello. That's the Green Lake store. It's about half a mile down the road from here. I work there summers. The Fergusons wrote us that you were coming the first of July, and they asked us to welcome you to Green Lake for them. Our place is directly across the lake, over there." He gestured in the direction of the opposite shore. Straining their eyes, the twins could see a figure of a small boy on the dock. "That's my little brother, Ralph. He's a good kid, when he's not getting into trouble."

T.J. grinned, and Claudia caught her breath. His shiny white teeth flashed behind a barricade of braces exactly like her own! Delighted, she relaxed the muscles of her mouth and returned an identical smile, much to her sister's amusement.

T.J. went on, "My folks would like you all to come to our big Fourth of July barbecue, about four o'clock. There'll be a lot of people there; so you can get acquainted with your summer neighbors. Green Lake may look deserted from here, but there are a bunch of houses hidden away in the woods. And, Mrs. Fletcher, Mom asked me to tell you that she's going to the food market in Andersville this morning. She thought maybe you'd like to go along and find out where things are. You don't want to buy all your stuff at the Green Lake store. The prices are out of sight."

The twins were stunned into silence by the barrage of good will. Their parents thanked T.J. for the invitation and accepted with pleasure. "Your parents must be close friends of the Fergusons," said Mr. Fletcher.

"You bet! We've been spending our summers here for, oh, I guess about ten years now."

"I've known Ned Ferguson about that long myself," Mr. Fletcher said.

"We'll certainly miss them around here this summer," T.J. said. Then he added hastily, "Of course, we're always glad to have some new faces around, especially friends of the Fergusons. This is the first time they've rented their cabin. I'm sure they'll have fun at the ocean, but it's too bad they took the cat. You'd have enjoyed fooling around with her."

"The cat?" Cassie repeated. "They took their cat to the ocean?"

"Sure, they're great in saltwater. They zip along like anything."

Claudia and Cassie exchanged glances. Since Claudia still didn't seem to be capable of speech, Cassie said, "I didn't know cats could swim. I mean, we have a cat at home, and he absolutely *hates* water."

T.J. threw back his head and laughed, causing his braces to glitter in the sun. "Not that kind of a cat! A catamaran, a two-hulled sailboat. I guess you're not so hot on sailing, huh?"

"True," agreed Mr. Fletcher. "Rowboats are more our speed. We seem to have inherited one, but the oars are a little peculiar. No two of them are the same length."

"Yeah, I know," T.J. said sympathetically. "If I were you, I'd patch up that cracked one and use it with the longer of the other two. You could do it with duct tape. I think my father has some."

Mr. Fletcher flashed a triumphant look at his daughters, then smiled at T.J. "That's exactly what I plan to do. And I have some of my own, but thanks anyway. Sure you won't join us for coffee?"

"No, I really have to go. I'm late already. Old man Weigel will throw a fit. See you around, OK?" T.J. walked down the steps toward his canoe. As he was untying it, he stopped and turned back. "What were you doing up there on the balcony this morning?" he asked, looking at Claudia. Then he blushed a bright red. "I wasn't really spying, but, well, I was curious about all of you, so I looked over, and . . ."

Claudia blushed herself, hesitating. Finally she said, "I was doing my exercises. If I don't

10

stretch out every day, my muscles get tied into knots. I didn't know anybody was watching."

"Claudia's a dancer," Cassie supplied.

T.J. said softly, "Hey, I'm sorry. I didn't mean to embarrass you. It was kind of neat, you know? You looked really graceful up there." He flipped the line into the canoe, then stepped in himself, regaining his seat with practiced ease.

"Well, I'll be seeing you. And welcome to the lake."

The Fletchers watched as T.J. paddled silently away, heading for a small stretch of beach a short distance to the right of their cabin.

"What a nice young man!" said Mrs. Fletcher enthusiastically.

Cassie nodded, unwilling to tear her eyes from the figure in the canoe.

"He *is* nice," Claudia said. She paused, then added in a small voice, "I wish he hadn't watched me doing my exercises, though."

"Oh, no!" wailed Cassie, causing her parents and Claudia to look at her inquiringly. "If he saw you in your bathing suit, he saw *me* in my pajamas! He's a peeping Tom, that's what he is!" But she didn't look terribly distressed.

"What do you suppose T.J. stands for?"

Mrs. Fletcher wondered as she went into the cabin to start scrambling the eggs.

"*T* for Tom, as in Peeping," suggested Mr. Fletcher. "And *J* for Just Looking Around."

"Oh, *Daddy!*" The girls groaned in unison.

Mrs. Fletcher's head appeared at the kitchen window. "I don't care what his name is, I think he's a lovely boy. It was very nice of his parents to send him over to make us feel at home, and I'll be delighted to go food shopping with Mrs. Howard. As for the Fourth, it sounds like great fun. We'll have to plan on having the Howards to dinner next week to reciprocate. Let's see, we could start with gazpacho, and then maybe marinated chicken . . ."

Mr. Fletcher, on his way to get the duct tape out of the car, interrupted with, "What if the senior Howards turn out not to share their son's charm? We might be stuck with a couple of losers. And what about the little brother? Maybe he's a holy terror. I don't recall T.J. mentioning any other siblings, but suppose there are seven more Howards waiting in the woods, ready to descend like vultures on your marinated chicken?"

"Oh, go get your silly tape!" Mrs. Fletcher said good-naturedly. "And hurry up, the eggs won't take long. The bacon's a little crisp, but it'll be all right."

Left alone on the deck, Cassie and Claudia continued to watch as T.J. lifted the canoe out of the water onto the beach, then disappeared among the trees up a path that presumably led to the Green Lake store.

"On a scale of one to ten, what do you think?" asked Cassie dreamily.

Claudia shrugged, absently twisting her ponytail. "Oh, maybe eight and a half."

"Oh, come on!" said her twin, rolling her eyes. "At least a nine!"

Claudia considered, the Mona Lisa look passing over her face. "OK, a nine. But he's not nearly as gorgeous as Mikhail Baryshnikov."

"But *almost* as gorgeous as John McEnroe before he hits the tennis court and gets all sweaty," Cassie countered.

Claudia shrugged again. "He probably has a girlfriend. Guys who look like that always have girlfriends."

Cassie grinned. "Well, for heaven's sake, we don't want to *marry* him! We're all just going to be friends, right?"

"Right," Claudia agreed. As they went into the cabin to help their mother bring out the

13

plates, she added softly, "But I still wish he hadn't watched me this morning."

"And I wish you'd woken me up sooner so I could have been decent," said Cassie. "And then, of course, there I was with my fat thighs hanging out!"

"And me with my braces," Claudia said. Then she smiled. "But he wears braces, too. I think that's pretty neat."

"Yeah."

The sisters smiled at each other, comfortable in the knowledge that, as usual, they were in perfect agreement.

Chapter Two

"Hey, what about that swim?" asked Claudia suddenly, pausing on the threshold of the kitchen. "I'm really dying to get into the water."

"No dice," said Mrs. Fletcher, pushing plates piled high with eggs and bacon at her daughters. "Breakfast is ready, and I'm not going to watch it get cold while you two swim. The water can wait until after we eat. We're going to be here an entire month."

"OK," said Claudia, taking a plate for herself and one for her father, who was just coming in the door with the tape. "Daddy, after you fix that oar, let's row over to the island. We could swim off the rocks from there."

"Fine by me," said Mr. Fletcher. "You know,

15

I could very easily become accustomed to the life of leisure."

"It's about time," said Mrs. Fletcher as she and Cassie followed Claudia and Mr. Fletcher out onto the deck. "It's been five years since you took a real vacation, and now that you've got the restaurant running smoothly, you deserve a rest. With Mrs. Thompson in charge, you've got nothing to worry about."

Mr. Fletcher grimaced. "True, but I can't help wondering about that new chef. He's excellent, but he strikes me as being the temperamental type. I just hope Mrs. Thompson can handle it if he causes any problems."

"Relax, Daddy," Cassie said cheerfully. "I'm sure that tough old lady can handle anything! And if she needs advice, she's got our number here. Mmmm, delicious breakfast, Mom."

"Why do you suppose food tastes so much better when you eat it outdoors?" wondered Claudia. "If my appetite keeps up like this, I'm bound to put on weight."

"Oh, stop it!" groaned her sister. "If there's one thing I can't stand, it's someone as slim as you worrying about gaining weight. If you put on a few pounds, I probably will too, and I'll end up looking like the back of a truck."

"That's ridiculous," Claudia said. "You've

16

got a fantastic figure. Look at me—I've got a dancer's body, which means no figure at all, not to mention these darned braces."

Mr. and Mrs. Fletcher exchanged glances. "Yes, you're really an ugly pair, you two," said Mr. Fletcher. "How do you suppose we produced such unattractive children, as gorgeous as we are?" he asked his wife, in mock despair.

"Beats me," she replied. "But considering they're all we've got, I guess we'll just have to make the best of it."

Just then a series of explosions echoed and re-echoed across the lake. Claudia dropped her fork, and Mrs. Fletcher choked on some coffee.

"If it's the Revolution, count me out," sputtered Mrs. Fletcher. "I'm on vacation."

"Firecrackers, I bet," said Cassie, considering and then virtuously rejecting a second piece of bread and jam. "Somebody's celebrating the Fourth of July three days early."

Mr. Fletcher peered out across the lake. "Looks like T.J.'s little brother is the culprit. I warned you, Lydia, don't say I didn't!"

"Oh, hush!" Mrs. Fletcher laughed. "Why is it, I wonder, that little boys seem to love things that make loud noises? If I'd had twin boys

17

instead of twin girls, I'd either be deaf by now or a nervous wreck—probably both!"

Another round of firecrackers exploded as the telephone began ringing. "And we came here for peace and quiet!" Mr. Fletcher sighed.

"I'll get it. Probably a wrong number," Mrs. Fletcher said as she went into the cabin. She was gone for several minutes while the girls and their father finished breakfast. When she returned, she was smiling. "That was Frieda Howard, to apologize for the noise and to say she'll be driving into town in about half an hour. She sounds like a lovely woman. She's going to pick me up; so if you're going to explore the island, you'll have to go without me. Guess I'd better change into something a little less casual. Girls, clear the table, will you?"

"I'll have this oar mended in a jiffy," said Mr. Fletcher. "Then we'll take off."

As the twins carried the dirty dishes into the kitchen, Claudia said to Cassie, "You know, we only arrived here last night, and already I feel as though we belong. Everyone's so friendly."

"Everyone?" teased Cassie, squeezing some dish detergent in the sink and soaping up the dishes. "You mean T.J. He's the only everyone we've met so far."

"OK, T.J. then." Claudia rinsed a plate and put it on the drainboard to dry. "I wonder if he works at the store every day. I'd hate to spend all my time at a beautiful place like this working indoors."

"What *I'm* going to be working on is my tan," said Cassie, frowning down at her pale legs. "If I have to be fat, I'd rather have brown fat than white fat."

"You are *not* fat!" Claudia said, whacking her twin lightly on the rear.

The girls quickly finished the dishes. Claudia went to the door to see if she could spot her father. "Hey, look, Daddy's got the boat out!"

Mr. Fletcher was seated in a rickety old rowboat that had once been painted white. "Welcome aboard the Dingy Dinghy," he called. "You'd better find something to bail with. It seems to be shipping water. And, Claudia, will you bring my hat? I think I left it on the kitchen counter. This sun is going to broil my bald spot."

Cassie found a small saucepan in the kitchen, and Claudia picked up their father's favorite sun hat, which, like the rowboat, was

19

somewhat worse for wear. "Daddy, I really think it's time you got a new hat," she said, stepping gingerly into the boat. "This one's had it."

"This hat," Mr. Fletcher intoned, settling it lovingly on his head, "is a family heirloom, and don't you forget it. Besides, I think it's appropriate for the captain of the Dingy Dinghy. Come on, Cass, hop to it!"

Cassie scrambled in, and the three Fletchers started off across the lake. Mr. Fletcher cut a rather crooked course until he got the hang of using two oars of different lengths. But soon the little boat was headed on a more or less direct line for the island in the middle of the lake.

"I wonder if the island has a name," said Cassie as she scooped water into the saucepan and poured it over the side.

"We'll have to ask T.J.," said Claudia. While Cassie and Mr. Fletcher chatted, Claudia thought about the boy they'd met that morning. He was attractive, all right, and certainly friendly. But Claudia wasn't sure how she felt about somebody, no matter how good-looking, who spied on people. She wasn't really sure if she liked him or not. No, that wasn't true. She *did* like him, and so did Cassie and her parents. What was it he'd said? *You looked real graceful up there.* Claudia blushed at the memory. At least she'd been wearing her new bikini instead of the old tank suit she'd almost put on. . . .

"Hey, Claude, wake up!" Cassie called over her shoulder from her seat in the prow. "We're almost to the island. What's the matter? You've hardly said a single word."

"Everything's fine," said Claudia, firmly putting T.J. out of her mind. "Look, there's a dock. We can tie up the boat while we go exploring."

Beneath the tall trees, the island's rugged terrain was cool and silent. Though it was deserted, discarded beer and soda cans gave evidence that many other explorers had been there before them. *Kids probably come to the island for parties at night,* Claudia mused. Had T.J. ever brought a girl there? she wondered. If he asked her, she'd go in a minute!

The twins and their father climbed over large, flat outcroppings of rock and found a perfect spot for swimming. Together, they launched themselves into the cool water of the lake. Then they returned to the rowboat, and this time Claudia and Cassie, side by side on the center seat, struggled with the oars while

21

Mr. Fletcher, his beloved hat still on his head, swam alongside, shouting encouragement.

When they finally reached their own dock, both girls were hot and sweaty, and so they jumped in the lake again. After the boat had been securely moored and Claudia and Cassie had had their dip, they flopped facedown on the sun-warmed dock, while Mr. Fletcher disappeared into the boathouse to tinker with the fishing poles he'd discovered earlier.

"I just love it here," Cassie mumbled, drowsy from the heat. "I hope we can come again next year."

"Me, too," Claudia agreed. "But we'll probably have jobs next summer."

She rolled over onto her back very carefully, to avoid getting splinters from the rough boards of the dock beneath her. She was dimly aware that she and Cassie ought to go up to their room and finish unpacking, since all they'd done the night before was dig out their nightclothes and tumble into bed, but at the moment it seemed too much like work. The sun beating down on her face made her see tiny dancing red pinwheels behind her lids.

What would she and Cassie be doing a year from now? she wondered sleepily. Maybe working in their father's restaurant as waitresses. Or maybe Cassie would get a job in the pro shop of the tennis club. She'd like that. She was such a sports nut.

Thinking about her twin, Claudia smiled. Cassie had always been a tomboy, swimming, playing softball, and starring on the high-school tennis team. She always seemed so sure of herself, never at a loss for words the way she herself was. As Cassie had said, she was subject to attacks of "the shys." Yet they were as close as two sisters could be, even sharing the same friends. Cassie was every bit as proud of Claudia's talent as a dancer as Claudia was of Cassie's athletic skills. They never fought the way other sisters did—or hardly ever. Maybe it had something to do with their being twins. *We sure are lucky,* Claudia mused as she drifted off into a doze.

The girls were awakened by the slamming of a screen door and the sound of voices inside the cabin.

"You must come and meet my family, Frieda," Claudia heard her mother say. Claudia sat up, rubbing her eyes. Cassie jumped to her feet at the same time, with a squawk of "Ouch!"

"What is it?" asked Claudia, peering groggily at her sister.

23

"Just a splinter," Cassie said. She limped over to a deck chair that was on the dock and began examining the sole of her right foot. "There it is, the little beast!"

"Need help?"

"No, I've got it." Cassie extracted the splinter and stood up gingerly as Mrs. Fletcher came out on the deck above them, accompanied by a pretty, slightly heavyset woman in a flowered shift with a pair of sunglasses pushed up on top of her head. Her hair, Claudia thought, was the same dark brown as T.J.'s, only straight.

"Girls? Come meet Mrs. Howard. Do you know where your father is?"

Just then Mr. Fletcher emerged from the boathouse, fishing poles in hand, and Cassie and Claudia followed him up the steps to the deck, where everyone was introduced. After a few moments of pleasant chat, Mr. Fletcher and the twins went out to Mrs. Howard's station wagon to unload the groceries.

"Any junk food?" Cassie asked hopefully, poking through one of the bags. She groaned when she lifted the heavy bag, but she brought it to the kitchen. The girls began putting the food away while their parents saw Mrs. Howard to her car.

"Frieda, you and Ben must come over and join us for drinks this evening," said Mrs. Fletcher. "And bring the boys, of course, if they don't have other plans."

"I'd love to, Lydia," said Mrs. Howard, "but our two eldest, Susan and Michael, are coming in from Albany this evening, which is where we're from, and we're meeting them at the bus depot. How about tomorrow night?"

"Fine," Mr. Fletcher said. "Around five?"

"Five it is. See you then." Mrs. Howard poked her head out the car window. "Nice meeting you, girls," she called to Cassie and Claudia, who had come out to say goodbye. "I hope to be seeing a lot of you this summer, and so does T.J. Bye!"

"She's just as nice as she sounded over the phone," said Mrs. Fletcher enthusiastically after Mrs. Howard had driven away. "There's a marvelous supermarket in Andersville, and she pointed out a wonderful little museum run by the local historical society. We'll have to go there one of these days. There's also a movie house and a Dairy Queen—all the comforts of home. And, Frank, Frieda tells me there's an excellent restaurant a few miles off in the woods, the Adirondack Inn. The own-

25

er's a friend of theirs. She thought you might like to meet him, compare notes."

"Sounds good," said Mr. Fletcher. "Anybody want to join me in testing out these fishing poles? I think I'll take the Dingy Dinghy out and see if I can catch anything. There ought to be bass in a lake like this."

"Thanks, Daddy, I think I'll pass," Claudia said, going back inside.

"Me, too," Cassie agreed, following her. "Mom, didn't you get any postcards? We want to send some to all the gang—Jody and Robin and Ken and Chuck," she counted on her fingers.

"Don't forget Marty, Christy, and Paul," Claudia reminded her. "And we ought to write cards to our grandparents."

"I never thought about postcards," Mrs. Fletcher admitted. "But I'm sure they must have them at the Green Lake store. Frieda says they carry just about everything, from kerosene to diapers. But she agrees with T.J. that the prices are pretty steep."

"How expensive can postcards be?" asked Cassie. "Let's walk up there after lunch, Claude, kind of check it out."

"Well, maybe," said Claudia, frowning slightly.

"Why maybe?" her twin asked. "Afraid T.J. will think we're chasing him?"

As usual, Cassie had read her mind. "Something like that," Claudia murmured.

Cassie sighed. "Honestly, Claude, it's a perfectly legitimate errand. We want postcards, the store sells them. Therefore, we go to the store to buy postcards. It's no big deal."

"I guess not." But Claudia wasn't completely convinced.

"Have you ladies unpacked your suitcases yet?" asked Mrs. Fletcher as she arranged fresh fruit in a bowl. The girls said they hadn't and went up the stairs to their bedroom.

There was only one closet—actually an alcove with a curtain in front of it—but since they'd brought mostly jeans, T-shirts, and bathing suits, that wasn't a problem. The drawers of the pine dresser would provide plenty of space.

"I wonder if Jody'll manage to snag Ken this summer," said Cassie, piling underwear and socks into the top drawer. "She told me that's going to be her major project."

"Not if Marty has anything to say about it," Claudia responded. "Marty's had her eye on

Ken for ages. Hey, leave some room for my stuff!"

"Yeah, but Jody's really determined. Do you know, he's the main reason she went on that crash diet, so that he'll notice her when the gang is hanging out at the pool?"

Claudia shook out a very wrinkled sundress and draped it over a hanger. "I hope there's an iron around here somewhere." She paused, frowning. "If Jody throws herself at Ken, Marty's going to be really miserable. I can't believe she'd risk losing her best friend over some dumb boy."

"Ken's not dumb," said Cassie. "And I bet lots of girls are going to be after him, now that he's got that lifeguard job, not just Jody and Marty."

"Maybe," Claudia folded several pairs of jeans neatly and put them in a drawer. "I think it would be awful, though, if Jody and Marty stopped being friends because of Ken. I'd really hate to see our gang break up over something like that."

"Yeah, I know. But it's bound to happen sooner or later, I guess. We'll probably all lose touch after next year when we go off to college."

Claudia was silent, thinking that even she and Cassie would be separated after their senior year, since Cassie had already decided on the University of Pennsylvania while she herself was hoping to win a dance scholarship to Connecticut College. She and her twin had never been apart in their entire sixteen years, and Claudia found it difficult to imagine life without Cassie at her side. She sat back on her heels and sighed, causing Cassie to look down at her questioningly.

"Cheer up," said her sister, guessing what was going on in her mind. "It'll take more than a few miles or some lifeguard with muscles to come between *us*!"

"You'd better believe it," Claudia said, smiling. She tossed a pile of T-shirts into the drawer and zipped up the now empty suitcase. "You know," she reflected, "it's funny. We like so many of the same people and things, but we've never both liked the same boy—I mean, romantically. Like, you had that crush on Rob last fall, and I couldn't understand what you saw in him."

"Oh, were you ever *right*!" Cassie moaned and shoved her empty suitcase under the bed. "Talk about muscles. Most of Rob's were in his head. And you spent the entire month before we left wondering if Wally the Wimp really liked you or if he only thought of you as a friend."

"Walter is *not* a wimp! He's sensitive, that's all. We had some very heavy conversations." Claudia grinned impishly. "And he kissed me goodbye the night before we came up here."

"He *didn't*!" Cassie shrieked. "How was it? I can't stand it! Did it make your toes curl?"

Claudia giggled. "Not really. As a matter of fact, it was kind of wimpy." Both girls whooped with laughter. Finally Claudia said, "I guess I'd better put him on my postcard list. He gave me his address."

"And I've got Rob's." Cassie scowled at her sister in mock severity. "I can't believe you didn't tell me *immediately* about Wally kissing you. We tell each other everything."

"Well, almost everything," said Claudia modestly. "Whew! It's hot in here. Let's go back down and take another swim. And after lunch, we'll check out the Green Lake store."

"Great!" said Cassie. "Maybe I'll have just one Twinkie before we swim."

"You will not!" shouted Claudia. "Don't you know that Twinkies go right to your thighs?"

Cassie slipped out the door, avoiding by inches the T-shirt that her sister flicked at the thighs in question.

Chapter Three

After lunch on the deck, Cassie jumped up from the picnic table bench where she had been sitting and stretched luxuriously. "Hey, Claude, how about going over to the store now?" She turned to her parents. "Want to come?"

"No, thanks," said Mrs. Fletcher, yawning. "I'm looking forward to settling down on the dock with one of my new books. I've done enough shopping for one day. What about you, Frank?"

"Not me. I've been trying to catch whatever fish live in this lake for hours, with no success. It's a good thing you bought that canned tuna," he said and laughed. "I'm exhausted. You girls go ahead. You might pick up a postcard or two for us. I ought to send one to Mrs. Thompson, just to let her know we got here all right."

Claudia and Cassie went into the house, carrying the paper plates and the remains of lunch. "Should we change?" asked Claudia as she dumped the garbage into the plastic pail. "I mean, do you think it would be OK if we just wore our bathing suits?"

"T.J. seemed to like yours," Cassie teased.

Claudia blushed. "Oh, come on, Cassie! Stop reminding me!"

"You can do what you like, but I'm putting on my jeans," said Cassie firmly.

"I guess I'll wear shorts."

Claudia followed her twin up the stairs, and in a few minutes they had pulled clothes on over their bathing suits. Standing in front of the mirror that hung over the pine dresser, Claudia undid the rubber band that held her ponytail and brushed her hair vigorously until it lay long and silky over her shoulders. She was about to twist it up into a knot when Cassie said, "Oh, leave it that way, Claude. You have such pretty hair."

"So do you," said Claudia. "I'll never understand why you decided to cut it."

Cassie shrugged. "We may not be identical

33

twins, but we're still a lot alike. I just wanted to look different. Besides, it's easier to manage when I'm swimming or playing tennis."

"We don't really look very much alike. I mean, no more than any other sisters do." Claudia looked at herself in the small mirror. "Maybe it's that we think alike." She giggled. "Maybe people can tell. OK, I'll leave my hair down." She made her Mona Lisa face.

Cassie smiled. "Come on, Claude! Braces are big here at Green Lake, remember?"

Claudia thought about T.J.'s silver-bound smile. If only she could smile the way he did and not worry about it! Well, she thought, at least she didn't have much longer to go. Her braces would be coming off in September, and then she would smile all the time.

"Want to take the rowboat?" Cassie asked as she stood on the deck next to Claudia.

"It's only about half a mile to the store," said Claudia. "We'll probably make better time walking down the road. If we took the boat, we'd spend hours trying to steer it in the right direction."

So the girls walked, looking at the various cabins along the way and wondering about the people who lived in them. The lake road was used only by those who were staying there, and so only a few cars passed them. They saw families with children enjoying themselves along the water's edge, but most of the houses were concealed by trees, snuggled against the mountains that rimmed Green Lake. A few hand-lettered signs pointed the way to the store, and soon they found themselves approaching it.

The store itself was set back from the road behind a row of gas pumps and a display of small sailboats, their brightly colored sails gleaming in the afternoon sun.

"That must be the place," said Cassie, pointing toward a weathered wooden building. There were cardboard boxes of fresh vegetables and fruits on the porch, and a few women in bathing suits or shorts were picking over the merchandise. Two little boys shoved coins into the soda machine and got ice cold ginger ales back.

Inside, the store was cool and dark after the blazing sunshine outside. Glass-enclosed counters displayed maple sugar candies that made Cassie's mouth water, and hand-carved souvenirs, while other cases were filled with cheese and cold cuts. The walls were covered with clothing, scuba and boating gear, and posters of Green Lake in all four seasons. Kerosene lanterns hung from the rafters, along with inflated rubber rafts, beach toys, and a small canoe.

"Look, Cass," said Claudia, fingering a stack of brightly colored T-shirts with the words Green Lake surrounded by a design of pine trees printed on them. "Aren't these cute?"

"Yeah, but look at the price!" Cassie replied, holding out a tag for her sister's inspection.

"Eight-fifty! Forget it! T.J. wasn't kidding when he said things were expensive here."

"Speaking of T.J., I wonder where he is?" Cassie peered around the store, and Claudia poked her sharply in the ribs.

"For Pete's sake, don't be so *obvious*!" she whispered. But she was searching, too, and she didn't see their new friend among the few people in the store. She did spot a rack of postcards, however, and went over to it, followed by Cassie. They chose cards for all their friends back home, plus several for their parents. "I wonder how much these are?" Cassie said. "If they're as overpriced as the T-shirts, we'll be broke."

"We'd better ask somebody. Only it's hard to

tell who works here and who's a customer," Claudia added.

"Well, there's someone who definitely works here," said Cassie, nodding at a boy in faded jeans and a Green Lake T-shirt who was stamping prices on a carton of canned goods. "Let's ask him."

Postcards in hand, the girls went down the narrow aisle and stopped beside the boy Cassie had pointed out. "Excuse me—" she began.

The boy looked up, brown eyes sparkling under a thatch of dark hair. A wide grin spread over his tanned face. He scrambled to his feet, bumping into a shelf as he stood up.

"Oh, look out!" Cassie cried. But her warning came too late. Cans of peas rolled in all directions. One landed solidly on Claudia's sandaled foot, and she gave a little squawk of surprise and pain.

"Oh, no!" the boy groaned, hastily bending over and snatching up the can that had wounded Claudia. "Don the Klutz strikes again. You OK? Listen, I'm really sorry!"

"It's all right," Claudia assured him, rubbing her aching toes. "Here, we'll help you pick these up."

She and Cassie joined the boy in picking up

the scattered cans, then stacking them neatly on the shelf. "You're *sure* you're OK?" he kept asking Claudia.

When the last can was in place, the boy straightened up, grinning sheepishly. "Thanks for lending a hand, or rather, four hands," he said. "I'm always doing dumb stuff like that. What did you want to ask me?"

"Oh, the postcards." Cassie wondered where she had put them and finally found them on top of a box of oatmeal. "We just wanted to ask how much these are," she said. "We didn't see a price."

"Fifteen cents each, two for a quarter," he responded promptly. "Or is it a quarter each, two for fifteen cents?"

The girls stifled their giggles and exchanged wry glances that said as plainly as words, *We've got a joker on our hands.*

"Seriously, no kidding, two for a quarter. When you get to know me better, you'll appreciate my sense of humor, I hope. I mean, I *hope* you'll appreciate me. You're *definitely* going to get to know me better," he said, looking for a brief second right at Claudia. "My name is Don, by the way."

Another glance flashed between the twins,

but they couldn't help smiling back at Don's cheerful grin.

"Hi, Cassie, Claudia. I see you've met my crazy friend." It was T.J. who spoke, coming up behind the girls.

"I might have known!" Don moaned in mock misery. "Anytime some winners show up, T.J. gets there first. It's the story of my life!" Turning to T.J., he said, "We've met, all right. And I made a big impression—on *her* foot." He nodded in Claudia's direction. "Which one did I maim, anyway? Claudia or Cassie?"

"I'm Claudia. She's Cassie," Claudia told him. "Please don't worry about my foot. I have another one," she said, laughing.

"The Fletchers are staying at the Fergusons' cabin for July," said T.J. "I stopped by this morning to say hello. They're coming to our Fourth of July blast."

"Great," Don said enthusiastically. "Are you from around here?" he asked the girls.

"No, we live in southern Pennsylvania. This is our first trip to the Adirondacks," Cassie said. "Green Lake is really beautiful. We love it already."

Claudia nodded in agreement, adding, "We usually go to the Jersey shore for two weeks in the summer. This is the first time in ages our father has been able to take a whole month off from work."

"Young man, would you please get one of those lanterns down for me? I can't reach it," complained an elderly gentleman whose knobby knees protruded from beneath a pair of brightly colored Bermuda shorts.

"Sure, right away," said Don. "I'll have to get the stepstool." He leaned over to Claudia and whispered conspiratorially, "Little does he know that I'll probably break the lantern *and* my neck! See you on the Fourth." He hurried off, leaving Claudia, Cassie, and T.J. laughing.

"On land, Don's got two left feet," T.J. said. "But put him in a sailboat or anything else that floats, and he's in his element. He wins every boat race on the lake. You'll see him in action in the Green Lake Regatta at the end of the month."

"Will you be entering the race?" Cassie asked.

"Oh, sure, but he'll beat me. Always has since we were ten years old. If you want to learn how to sail, Don's the guy to teach you. But you'll have to ask him. He's too shy to volunteer."

"Shy!" cried both girls in unison.

"I know, he's always cracking jokes, but that's just a cover-up. Girls kind of scare him. He's afraid they'll laugh at him because he's so clumsy, and so he acts like a clown. He's a great guy, though."

"I like him," said Claudia, smiling, "even if he did almost ruin my dancing career."

"That's right, you're a dancer. What kind? Ballet?" T.J. asked.

Claudia shook her head. "No, modern, like Martha Graham or Merce Cunningham."

"Never heard of them," said T.J. Turning to Cassie, he asked, "Do you dance, too?"

"No way! I'm the family jock," she told him.

"She's on the tennis team at school and the swimming team, too," Claudia said proudly. "And she's a great basketball player, even though she's short."

"Hey, fantastic!" said T.J. "I'm on the tennis team at my school, too. Or I *was*. I graduated in June. There are some decent courts over at the lake club. Want to play one of these days?"

"I'd love it," said Cassie, beaming.

"How about Friday morning? I have the day off. It would be really fun. A lot of the kids hang out at the club."

"Claudia plays, too," Cassie said, glancing

41

over at her sister, hoping she didn't feel left out.

"I'm not nearly as good as Cassie," said Claudia quickly.

"I'll take you both on. Two against one. Or better yet, I'll ask Don to come along. Believe it or not, those two left feet function pretty well on a tennis court. It's only complicated things like walking that foul him up."

"T.J.! Pumps!" A loud voice boomed through the store.

T.J. sighed. "No rest for the weary. In case you're wondering, that means there's somebody outside who wants gas. Got to go. See you."

Claudia and Cassie followed him down the grocery aisle, watching admiringly as he cleared the porch steps with one bound, heading for the gas pumps and a waiting van. Then they took their postcards to the antique cash register, where a plump, red-haired girl, her face and arms a mass of freckles, rang up the sale. "Friends of T.J.'s?" she asked, smiling as she dropped the cards into a brown paper bag.

"Well, yes, I guess so. We just met him this morning," said Cassie. "We arrived last night. I'm Cassie Fletcher, and this is my sister, Claudia."

"The Fergusons' place, right?" the girl said. "I'm Pat Murphy. My folks' place is three cabins north of yours. I guess I'll be seeing you around. You going to the Howards' Fourth of July barbecue?"

"Yes, are you?" Claudia asked.

"Sure. Everybody'll be there. It'll be a good chance for you both to meet people. There are always a lot of kids around." A loud crash from the back of the store caused all three girls to jump. Then Pat laughed, shaking her head. "That has to be Don! Has he run into you yet?"

Claudia and Cassie nodded, laughing too. "He seems to be accident-prone," said Claudia, wiggling her toes and wincing.

"*Disaster*-prone is more like it. Well, see you on the Fourth," said Pat as she turned to the next impatient customer.

After the dimness of the store, the sunshine made Cassie and Claudia blink. They waved at T.J., who waved back from behind the van. Then they started down the dusty road.

"I think T.J. really likes you," said Claudia, glancing over at her twin.

"I think T.J. likes everybody," Cassie countered. "He's just a naturally friendly person.

And Don's funny and nice. But, oh, Claudia, wouldn't that be incredible?" Cassie said and smiled. "I mean, if T.J. liked me. I'm looking forward to a very interesting vacation!"

Chapter Four

When Cassie and Claudia arrived home, their parents whisked them away on an exploratory drive around the area. They discovered a stable, where the girls immediately decided they must rent horses as soon as possible, and a small amusement park on the banks of another lake a few miles away.

By the time they had returned and eaten a leisurely supper on the deck, the sun was going down in a crimson blaze. The twins leaned side by side over the railing, looking out across the water.

"Is that the Howards' cottage?" asked Cassie, peering through the dusk. Some lights twinkled approximately where T.J.'s little brother had set off his fireworks that morning.

"Don't know," said Claudia dreamily. How dark and mysterious the opposite shore looked under the darkening sky, she thought. She could hardly see the island now. It blended into the night, a darker blur against the purplish sky. Somewhere down the lake, a radio or stereo was playing, and the music drifted faintly to her ears like a melody from another world. Every so often, she would hear a fish leaping out of the water or a night bird crying in the distance.

"It's so peaceful and romantic," she whispered softly.

"Look!" Cassie whispered back. "There's the evening star, right over that tall pine tree on the island." The pinpoint of light looked like an ornament on the top of a shadowy Christmas tree.

"Let's make a wish," said Claudia, "our first wish at Green Lake." She thought a moment, then said, "I wish we could stay here all summer."

Cassie sighed happily. "I can't think of a single thing to wish for! I feel as though I have everything I'll ever want right this minute."

Claudia smiled. "I know what you mean. Maybe you'd better save your wish for another night."

"Still, it seems a pity to waste a perfectly good wishing star," said Cassie. She looked up at the sky. "I wish—I wish—Darn! I wish these mosquitoes would stop eating me alive!"

Both girls burst into giggles as Cassie smacked at an insect on her arm. "Ouch!" she cried. "I must have gotten a sunburn today. All of a sudden, I can feel it."

"Then it's probably nine o'clock," said Claudia. The girls had a theory, proved over many summers and by many sunburns, that no matter what time of day you sunbathed, your skin would begin to tingle around nine o'clock that night.

"I'm going to find some sunburn cream," Cassie announced. "Coming?"

Claudia nodded, scratching a mosquito bite on her neck, and followed Cassie into the house.

Mr. and Mrs. Fletcher were absorbed in a game of checkers when their daughters entered the living room. "Cassie, dear, you look very pink, and so do you, Claudia," said Mrs. Fletcher, glancing up. "The sunburn stuff is on the bathroom shelf, next to the toothpaste. I used some myself a little while ago. You'd both better put some on. You don't want to peel."

47

"Who's winning?" asked Claudia, bending over her father's chair. It was a useless question since she could see that most of Mr. Fletcher's men had been removed from the board and were neatly stacked on Mrs. Fletcher's side.

"She is," said Mr. Fletcher, scowling. "Your mother is a checker wizard."

"Never mind, Daddy," Cassie soothed, patting him on his bald spot. "You'll cream her next time."

"Of course he won't," Mrs. Fletcher said. "This is the one game I can beat your father at, and I'm not about to retire as checkers champ. Watch this!" In three deft movements with one of her kings, she removed all but two of her husband's men from the board.

"Vicious, that's what she is. Anybody for Parcheesi?" asked Mr. Fletcher mournfully.

Cassie and Claudia laughed, heading for the stairs. "No, thanks," said Claudia. "Not tonight. We're pooped. Maybe tomorrow night."

Mrs. Fletcher shook her head. "The Howards are coming over tomorrow night, no Parcheesi then." She turned her attention back to the checkerboard.

As they went up the steps, Cassie said, "I

wonder if T.J. will be coming with Mr. and Mrs. Howard. That would be terrific."

Claudia shook her head. "I doubt it. But you're right. It would be terrific."

After slathering one another with sunburn lotion and brushing their teeth, the girls got into their nightclothes. Then Cassie went to the bureau and took out her diary. "I missed last night," she explained. "I made a New Year's resolution that I was going to make an entry every single day this year. I have to catch up."

"You're so good about that, Cass," said Claudia and sighed. "I gave up months ago. It got so boring writing down, 'Went to school, went to dance class, had spaghetti for dinner, hung out with the gang.' But you always have so much to say."

As Cassie climbed up the top bunk, she said, "It's fun. I keep thinking about how my children and grandchildren will be able to read about what I was doing way back in 1984. It's kind of a historical record, you know?"

"I'm going to read," Claudia informed her, grabbing a well-worn copy of *Jane Eyre* and snuggling down into her bunk. "That is, if I can keep my eyes open."

49

Lying on her stomach, the diary open in front of her, Cassie chewed on the end of her ballpoint pen, then began.

July 2, 1984

We arrived at Green Lake last night after an endless drive. Claudia and I were tied in knots from sitting in the car so long, and I could hardly stagger up the stairs to the bedroom we'll be sharing for the rest of the month.

The first thing that happened this morning was that a *very* attractive boy arrived at our dock in a canoe to say hello. He'd been watching Claudia do her dance exercises on the balcony from his cabin across the lake, and Claude was *hideously* embarrassed!! His name is T.J. Howard. I've been wondering what his real name (real names?) is (are?).

He works at the Green Lake store, and of course, Claude and I absolutely *had* to buy some postcards to send to our friends back home, so we went up there this afternoon. We met a friend of his, a really funny guy named Don. Don's nice-looking, but as T.J. says, he has two left feet.

He almost *crippled* Claudia by dropping a can of peas on her foot!

Claudia says she thinks T.J. likes me. I think she's being silly, but it sure would be nice if he did. Both Claude and I think he's neat. And I think Don likes Claude, so there are all sorts of possibilities this summer!

Cassie finished her entry by telling about their sightseeing trip that afternoon, and when she was through, she dangled the diary over the side of the bunk, saying, "Want to read what I wrote?"

"Hmmm?" Claudia's voice sounded sleepy, but she reached up to take the diary. There was a brief silence while she read, then a muffled explosion. "Don never showed that he liked me! You made that up!"

"Sure he did," said Cassie brightly. "I could tell, even though he didn't say anything. When you're finished, stick my diary in the drawer, will you? I'm going to sleep."

Cassie punched her pillow into a ball and nuzzled into it. There was no need for blankets or even a sheet. It was still very warm in the little bedroom, even though a cool breeze wafted in from the half-opened door to the balcony. A few minutes later, Claudia got out of the lower bunk and padded to the dresser, where she put away the diary. Then she turned out the light and called, "Night, Cass."

"Night, Claude."

But though both girls were tired from their eventful day, neither could fall asleep immediately. Each tossed and turned in her bunk, thinking.

Suddenly Cassie sat up. "Thomas Jefferson!" she shouted.

"George Washington!" Claudia shouted back. "What is this, some kind of game?"

"That's what T.J. stands for! Thomas Jefferson Howard. I'm sure of it!"

"No way," Claudia stated. "If that were his name, they'd call him Tom or Jeff. No, I figure it has to be something really far out like Thaddeus Jeremiah."

Cassie considered. "You may be right. How about Theodore Jehosophat?"

A giggle came from the lower bunk. "That's a good one. But then, you ought to be good at figuring out somebody's real name—Clarissa!"

Cassie rolled over and hung her head over the side, glaring at her twin, though she knew Claudia couldn't see her expression in the dark. "Don't you dare tell anybody, you rat!" she cried.

More giggles. "Of course not, sister dear! Or at least . . ." Claudia's voice trailed off tantalizingly.

"Or at least what?" asked Cassie suspiciously.

"Or at least not unless T.J. tells us *his* real name. Deal?"

"Well . . ." Cassie thought about it a minute, then said, "Deal. But you can't force him to tell."

"Who me? Force somebody to do something? I'm the shy one, remember?" Claudia yawned. "Hey, I'm really exhausted. Are you going to quiet down and let me go to sleep?"

Cassie echoed her yawn. "Yep. See you in the morning."

But before she dozed off, she thought, *Thomas Jefferson. That has to be it.* Remembering T.J.'s warm brown eyes, she smiled and closed her own.

The following morning was spent doing lovely, lazy vacation things like swimming, sunning, reading, and wandering through the woods collecting wildflowers. Claudia tried out a new pearly pink nail polish on her toenails and managed to persuade her sister to try some too.

After a leisurely lunch, Mr. Fletcher drove the twins to the stable they'd discovered, and the three rented horses for a pleasant hour's ride along woodland trails. Mrs. Fletcher stayed home to finish reading a novel and to prepare for their guests, though Claudia and Cassie couldn't see that much preparation was needed. The main question in both their minds was whether or not T.J. would join his parents. When they got back, they had another swim, then went upstairs to dress.

"Might as well look our best, just in case," said Cassie, and Claudia didn't need to ask in case of what.

But when Mr. and Mrs. Howard arrived, they said that all their children were otherwise occupied, though T.J. had sent his best.

"He probably has a date," Claudia said as she and Cassie went into the kitchen to bring out the hors d'oeuvres their mother had prepared.

"What do you suppose kids do on dates up here?" Cassie wondered.

"Oh, maybe go to the amusement park or the movies. Or maybe they just hang out at the lake club T.J. was telling us about," Claudia replied. "I hope we get to find out!"

The girls grinned at each other, then went out onto the deck to join their parents and the Howards, who were deep in conversation. Mr. Howard was tall and lanky, with gray hair that emphasized his tan and intensely blue eyes.

"Paul Newman," Cassie whispered to Claudia, who nodded in agreement. "Good looks seem to run in the family!"

Ben Howard, they learned, had grown up in the area. He had an endless fund of stories about Green Lake and the surrounding towns, which all the Fletchers found fascinating.

Suddenly the roar of a motorboat engine cut into the quiet conversation. It wasn't the first motorboat that had skimmed across the lake's surface, but this one appeared to be heading straight for the Fletchers' dock.

"Omigosh!" cried Cassie, leaping to her feet. "What does that nut-job think he's doing?"

The others joined her by the deck railing, and Mrs. Howard, shading her eyes against the slanting rays of the late afternoon sun, said calmly, "I believe that 'nut-job' is my son showing off."

Sure enough, as the speeding boat drew

nearer, Claudia and Cassie could see T.J. at the helm. Behind him, expertly cutting back and forth across its wake, was a water-skier who looked very much like Don. Just as the boat seemed in imminent danger of crashing into the dock, it veered away, and both boys waved, grinning like demons. They quickly became two diminishing specks on the shimmering water and were soon lost to view behind the island.

"It never ceases to amaze me that Don Lanser can't walk across a room without falling over his feet or breaking something, and yet he's such a whiz at water sports," Mrs. Howard said, sinking back into her deck chair.

Cassie and Claudia described their encounter with Don at the Green Lake store. Claudia stuck out her bruised foot as evidence.

During the rest of the Howards' visit, Cassie kept surreptitiously glancing out over the lake, hoping to catch another glimpse of T.J.'s boat, but the boys did not return. *Probably showing off for some other girls*, she thought. But she smiled happily at the thought that they'd come by.

By the time the Howards left, they and the twins' parents had become fast friends, and

Mrs. Fletcher had promised to bring her special deviled eggs to the barbecue the following day.

"It's going to be a really great party, Claude, I just know it!" said Cassie as she and her twin carried the glasses and empty hors d'oeuvre trays back into the cabin. "Didn't I tell you it was going to be a fantastic vacation?"

Chapter Five

"Do I look all right?" Cassie asked anxiously, presenting herself for Claudia's inspection. The twins had decided to reverse roles for the Howards' barbecue. Cassie was wearing Claudia's light blue sundress with the halter neckline, and Claudia had on new white pants and a bright green tailored blouse of Cassie's. Cassie had scooped her hair back on one side with a flowery barrette, and Claudia's long blond hair was tied with a green ribbon so that it cascaded over one shoulder.

"Terrific!" Claudia pronounced. "You ought to wear skirts more often, Cass. That dress does absolutely nothing for me, but with your figure, you look really great. T.J.'ll love it," she added with a giggle.

Cassie pretended to scowl, but she was secretly pleased. She leaned close to the little mirror. After a moment's consideration, she decided that she *did* look pretty good. "And you look fantastic. What I wouldn't give to have hips like yours!"

"What hips? These pants are *big* on me. It's a good thing they're not supposed to be tight-fitting."

"That's what I mean, bean-brain!" Cassie touched a little lip gloss to her mouth, something she didn't ordinarily do. "Well, I guess we're as ready as we'll ever be. We'd better go downstairs. Daddy will be having fits. You know how he is about getting places on time."

"Yeah, I know." But Claudia was in no hurry to join their impatient parents. "All of a sudden, I kind of wish we weren't going," she admitted.

"Oh, Claude! This is a fine time to have an attack of the shys!"

"I know, but I can't help feeling this way. The only people we know are T.J. and his folks. There'll be lots of other people we *don't* know." Claudia took Cassie's place at the mirror and gave a tentative Mona Lisa smile. "What if they don't like us?"

"What's there not to like?" But Cassie sympathized with her sister's reluctance and added, "Claudia, come on! We're going to a party. It's going to be fun, like being with our gang at home."

"That's at home," said Claudia softly. "This is different."

"Sure it's different. Who knows, it may be better. And don't you *dare* say it may be worse! Besides, we know Don and Pat, so that makes five people who won't be strangers."

"Hey, ladies! Get a move on!" their father's voice boomed up the stairs. "Your mother's deviled eggs are starting to congeal!"

Claudia looked at Cassie, forcing a smile. "OK, I'm ready, I guess."

"That's more like it! We're going to knock 'em, dead, Claude, just you wait and see!"

The Howards' place was overflowing with guests when the Fletchers arrived. Teenagers, children, and adults mingled happily. Mr. Howard, in a huge white apron with red letters that said BURGER BURNER, presided over three smoking braziers on which chicken, hot dogs, and hamburgers sizzled. Introductions were made all around, though the twins could only catch about half the names that were tossed at them. Somewhere in the kaleidoscope of faces they were able to single out T.J.'s older sister and brother, Susan and Michael. The cheerful ten-year-old who almost set fire to Cassie's dress with a handful of sparklers could only have been Ralph. He begged Cassie to come see his bug collection and refused to take no for an answer. Finally Cassie gave in and followed him, holding onto his sticky little hand. She threw Claudia a look as Ralph dragged her away. "The wrong Howard boy seems to be interested in me," she whispered to her sister.

Claudia felt a little nervous at being left alone in the crowd of strangers, so she was very relieved when Don made his way toward her.

"How's your foot?" he asked.

"Just fine, thanks. Please don't worry about it," she said. "Hey, you're a great water-skier. But we almost had heart attacks when you two came by yesterday."

Don grinned sheepishly. "That was T.J.'s idea. We didn't really scare you, did we?"

Claudia smiled her tight-lipped smile. "Not once we knew it was you. But at first we thought you were going to blast right through the dock!"

Claudia felt a warm hand on her shoulder,

and she turned to see T.J. smiling at her. She noticed again that he didn't make any effort to conceal his braces. Almost imperceptibly, her lips relaxed, and she returned his smile.

"Hey, is this guy trying to break your other foot?" he said, laughing. "You have to watch out for him. He'll do anything for a joke."

Don sighed dramatically. "We jokers are a misunderstood lot," he said. Then he sniffed the air like a hunting dog. "Do I smell the famous Howard barbecued chicken?" He clutched at his stomach and grimaced comically. "Lemme at it!" And he disappeared into the group clustered around the braziers, leaving Claudia alone with T.J.

"I asked Susan about those people you mentioned the other day," T.J. said.

"What people?" asked Claudia, mystified.

"Those dancers, Martha Graham and Merce Cunningham. She's into cultural stuff like that. She told me that Martha Graham's a great old lady who revolutionized modern dance and that Merce Cunningham has a fantastic dance company. I guess you must have thought I was really stupid, not knowing who they were."

Claudia shook her head vigorously. "Oh, no. I mean, if you don't follow modern dance, you probably wouldn't know them. Most people don't. Even Cassie gets mixed up sometimes."

Speaking of Cassie made Claudia wonder where her sister was. She spotted her out on the Howards' dock, talking animatedly to several kids Claudia had never seen before. *I wish I could do that,* she thought, *talk to perfect strangers as though I'd known them all my life.*

"So, that's what you want to do, be a modern dancer?" T.J. persisted.

"Well, I'd like to, but I'm not good enough yet," Claudia answered, turning her attention back to him. Their eyes met, and she was mesmerized by how intense T.J.'s were. "Maybe someday . . ." Her voice trailed off.

"Look, I'm really sorry I spied on you that first day," said T.J., his words coming out in a rush. "But it wasn't really spying. I was just curious about the new people on the lake. I'm sorry if I embarrassed you."

"That's all right," Claudia said. "I mean it." And as she spoke, she knew it was true. All of a sudden, she didn't feel shy anymore, just comfortable and happy. T.J. was so nice and good-looking, and he'd actually taken the time to find out about something that interested her. Did that mean he cared about her? *Don't be silly, Claudia,* she told herself sternly. *He's interested in Cassie, not you. He's just being polite.* But the glow remained, lighting up her face and making her eyes sparkle.

"Maybe tomorrow morning I'll just take my father's binoculars and spy on *you* for a change," she teased, amazed to find that the words came so easily to her.

T.J. threw back his head and laughed. "Fair enough! But don't be surprised if you find me staring back!"

"Claude! Come meet Freddie and Lois and Charlie!" cried Cassie, coming up behind Claudia and putting her arm around her twin's waist. "Hi, T.J., how's it going?"

"Couldn't be better. Where've you been?"

"Your brother Ralph seems to have taken a liking to me. He just showed me every bug he's ever caught. If you hadn't been so absorbed in conversation with my little sister, you might have noticed and come and saved me."

"*Little* sister!" said T.J. "What do you mean?"

"She's ten minutes older than I am," Claudia told him, glancing over to catch Cassie's eye. But Cassie's entire attention was focused on T.J., and she didn't look away. Claudia suddenly felt abandoned, as though her sister had somehow betrayed her. But that was silly. Cassie's arm was still around her waist.

"I'm starved," Claudia said brightly. "Don's right. The smell of that chicken is irresistible. Want to eat, Cass?"

"Sure. I told Freddie and Lois and Charlie that we'd eat with them. You coming, T.J.?" Cassie asked.

"Why not?" T.J. smiled. "But first tell me what your real name is. Cassie has to be short for something, like Cassandra, maybe."

Cassie shot a glance at Claudia that said, *Remember our deal?*

Claudia felt a blush creeping over her face. "Uh, well, yes, you're right, T.J. It's kind of a pet name. Cass doesn't much like her real name."

"Boy, I can understand that!" T.J. sighed. "I have the same problem. I'm named for both my grandfathers—Theodore and Jeremiah! How do you like that?"

Cassie gave Claudia a squeeze that almost knocked the breath out of her. "We were both right!" she said happily. "Claude picked Jeremiah, and I picked Theodore!"

"What is this, some kind of a bet?" asked T.J., looking from one girl to the other. But he didn't seem in the least annoyed, much to Claudia and Cassie's relief.

"Not exactly," murmured Claudia. "It's just that Cass and I were wondering what T.J. stood for, and we figured it had to be something really—"

"Awful, right?" T.J. was laughing, his braces shining in the sunlight.

"Not awful, exactly. More unusual." Cassie giggled, and Claudia nodded.

"You said you'd tell," Claudia reminded her sister softly, and Cassie caught her eye.

"OK, here goes. *My* real name is . . ." Her voice faltered, and it seemed as though she'd never get out the hated name.

"Clarissa!" Claudia pronounced triumphantly.

T.J. didn't seem disturbed. "What's so terrible about that?" he asked innocently. "Clarissa is kind of—well, kind of old-fashioned. And it's pretty. I never knew a girl named Clarissa before."

Cassie beamed. "Well, *Theodore*, now that that's settled, how about some of that chicken?"

"Clarissa, my dear, I'm with you!"

T.J. offered his arm to Cassie, which she took, laughing up at him. But then he paused and offered his other arm to Claudia, and the three of them marched off to the barbecue, both girls glowing.

"I'm positively *stuffed*," Cassie groaned half an hour later, as she and Claudia relaxed in canvas deck chairs on the Howards' dock. "Why didn't you stop me when I took a hot dog and a burger after I'd had the chicken?"

"Because I didn't want to be known as the only pig at this party," Claudia joked. "Take it easy, Cass. You'll work it off swimming and hiking, not to mention playing tennis on Friday."

"I hope you're right." Cassie sighed. "I can just feel my thighs ballooning under this skirt!"

"My waistband feels a little tight, too—"

"If you complain about gaining weight, I'll *kill* you!"

T.J. had taken off to help his father and brothers assemble the fireworks that would form the finale of the celebration. The girls sat in comfortable silence, content to watch the sun sinking slowly behind the mountains that ringed the lake.

T.J.'s so handsome, and such fun, Cassie thought. *I think Claude's right. He really does like me. I wonder what it would be like to kiss him. . . .*

At the same time Claudia was thinking, *He likes Cassie, I can tell, I guess he likes me too, but not the way a boy likes a girl he wants to date. He and Cassie have so much in common. He and I have nothing in common at all. I'm not a jock, like Cassie, or funny and easy to talk to, the way she is. But still, he did take the trouble to find out about what interests me. . . .*

"Hi, twins!" It was Don, plunking himself down between their chairs, his infectious grin spreading over his face. "Contrary to popular expectations, I didn't dump my food in anyone's lap or knock anybody into the lake. So you can talk to me in perfect safety. Amazing meal, huh? I ate enough for ten people."

Cassie laughed, clutching her stomach. "You said it! If you knocked me into the lake now, I think I'd sink like a stone!"

"Me, too." Claudia giggled. "But I can't think of a better way to go."

"Right, full of good food, surrounded by good friends," said Don.

"Oh, look!" cried Claudia, pointing up at the sky where the first of the fireworks was exploding against the twilight. A glowing

68

rosette blossomed, then faded, showering sparks upon the lake. Breathless ooohs and aaahs greeted the brilliant lights, and immediately another firecracker shot up into the air, flowering above their heads.

As the darkness of evening closed in, the fireworks became more brilliant, and all the guests gathered on the shore to marvel at the sight. Each flash of light was duplicated in the still waters of the lake. Cassie got up from her chair and went with Don to the very edge of the shore, leaving Claudia behind. Claudia didn't mind. She was completely wrapped up in the beauty of the blazing colored lights against the darkening sky.

"Pretty, isn't it?" T.J. settled down next to her.

"I thought you were supposed to be down there shooting them off," said Claudia.

"I did my bit setting them up. Now I can sit back and enjoy it." He wrapped his arms around his knees, looking upward. "Where's Cassie?"

"She went down to the water with Don." Claudia tried to meet his eyes, but the off-and-on glimmer of the fireworks made it difficult. Was he searching for Cassie? She couldn't tell. "It's a great Fourth of July party," she said softly. "Thanks for asking us."

"I didn't ask you, my parents did," he said truthfully. "But I'm glad they did. I'm glad you came, Claudia. And Cassie, too."

Claudia had an almost irresistible urge to reach out and touch T.J.'s dark brown hair. Instead, she reached down and patted the big golden retriever that had followed him to where she sat. The dog looked up at her, his long pink tongue lolling in a friendly fashion.

"What's his name?" she asked, scratching his silky ears.

"Sundance, short for the Sundance Kid," T.J. replied, slapping the dog gently on the back. Sundance immediately rolled over, all four paws in the air, and T.J. scratched his belly. "Only he's not much of a kid anymore. He's a pretty old guy now."

Three rockets shot upward through the velvet darkness, forming chrysanthemums of red, gold, and green, and Claudia gasped involuntarily. Then she noticed that the first star of the evening had appeared in the sky, though it was somewhat outdone by the fireworks display. She remembered Cassie's words of the night before. *I can't think of a single thing to wish for*, she'd said. *I feel as*

70

though I have everything I'll ever want right this minute. That was exactly the way Claudia felt at that moment. She suddenly wanted Cassie with her to share her perfect contentment, and as though the wishing star had answered her, two dim figures appeared, coming toward her.

"Isn't it gorgeous!" Cassie bubbled, dropping down beside T.J. in the grass, her dress billowing around her like the petals of a dark flower. "It's the best fireworks display I've ever seen—and only one minor casualty!"

"Minor!" Don flopped down beside her, waving a hand plastered with Band-Aids. "Sure, it's minor to *you!* You didn't have your hand almost blown off by a dud! Hey, T.J., what happened to you? Your dad drafted me to take your place, which as you can see was very unwise. You owe me one, buddy!"

T.J. laughed, clapping Don on the shoulder. "Hey, it was bound to happen! You're the one who's accident-prone, not me." Then his voice became serious and concerned. "You OK? I mean, it's nothing serious, is it?"

Don shook his head. "No, just a little powder burn. I'm fine."

Cassie moved next to Claudia, saying, "You're awfully quiet. What's up?"

"I'm just enjoying everything. I was wondering where you were," Claudia responded, smiling.

"I'm right here, dummy!" Cassie joined T.J. in rubbing Sundance's belly. "Isn't he a great dog? And isn't this a great party?"

"Sure is." Claudia sighed.

A final burst of fireworks brightened the night sky, as one rocket after another exploded above the lake. After the last fiery blossom had faded and died, the observers down by dock began to trail back up to the house, chatting and laughing. Cassie smacked at a mosquito on her bare shoulder. "Horrible little creature!" she muttered. "We should have brought the repellent. Oh, well, nothing's perfect, I guess."

But some things almost are, thought Claudia.

Then somebody lit torches here and there around the grounds, bringing faces into sharp focus. Claudia watched T.J. bending down to talk to Cassie, and Cassie's bright, pretty face looking up at him as though he were the only person in the world. *He belongs to Cassie,* she thought, and the bubble of happiness within her seemed to deflate, leaving her conscious of the fact that the air had cooled and that the mosquitoes were searching for other prey. She caught Don's eye and smiled stiffly. "Maybe we'd better go in," she said, standing up.

Later that night, Cassie wrote for a few minutes in her diary before going to sleep. Claudia was barely awake when her sister's hand, holding the book, waved before her nose. She took it, almost reluctantly, and focused on the words in Cassie's neat handwriting.

This has been absolutely the best Fourth of July ever! We went to the Howards' barbecue and made total pigs of ourselves, or at least Claude and I did. I can't speak for Mom and Dad. It seemed like the whole population of Green Lake was there. But most important, T.J. was there. I've decided I'm madly in love with him, and I think Claudia is, too. He's the handsomest, nicest boy either of us has ever met. His friend, Don the Klutz, is OK, too, and lots of fun, but not *nearly* as fantastic as T.J.

The day after tomorrow we're playing tennis, Claude and me, T.J., and Don. I

can hardly wait! Happy Fourth of July—
and fifth and sixth, seventh, and eighth,
etc.

Claudia closed the diary thoughtfully, then
after a brief silence, said, "Cass?"

"Hmmm?" her sister mumbled.

"Did you mean what you wrote about being
madly in love with T.J.? Or were you—kind of
exaggerating?"

Silence from the upper bunk. Finally: "I said
we were *both* madly in love with him. Care to
comment on that, Miss Fletcher?"

Claudia frowned. "You haven't answered my
question. Come on, Cass!"

"And you haven't answered *mine*! Night,
Claude."

"Night, Cass," Claudia responded softly, as
she got up and turned out the light.

Chapter Six

"Out! Sorry, Cassie. Score's thirty-forty," T.J. called, sending the tennis ball back across the net with a long, easy forehand stroke.

"Nuts!" wailed Cassie, glancing apologetically over at Don.

"Don't let it throw you, Cassie," he said over his shoulder, flashing a cheerful grin. "Let's try for deuce! We'll show them!"

Cassie rubbed the sweat out of her eyes with her forearm as she positioned herself for what might well be her final serve. Claudia crouched opposite her on the other side of the net, eyes sparkling. T.J., at the baseline, was watching her every move. It was the final game of the deciding set. Cassie and Don had won the first, T.J. and Claudia had taken the second and were leading in the third, five games to four. For an instant, a cool breeze off the lake ruffled Cassie's wet hair. Then, once again, the sun was beating down mercilessly on the club's tennis courts. Cassie bounced the ball a few times, then tried to psych herself into feeling like Chris Evert Lloyd as she tossed it high in the air, slamming down with her racquet, aiming for the outside corner of T.J.'s court. It was in! He returned it with a good clean shot that barely cleared the net. Don sent it back to Claudia, who used her two-handed backhand to send it sailing into the far corner of Cassie's court. Taken off-stride, Cassie recovered and ran like mad, extending her racket at arm's length to send it back—and missed.

"Aargh!" she groaned as the ball bounced harmlessly out of her reach against the wire netting and then rolled right up to her feet. Cassie yowled in rage and kicked the fuzzy yellow ball as far as she could, tossing her racket in the air.

"Hey, cool it, partner," said Don, throwing an arm around her shoulders. "We made them fight for every point. You're a dynamite tennis player! We'll beat them easily next time."

"Good game!" Claudia called from the opposite court, coming to the net with hand outstretched, closely followed by T.J. Cassie slogged to the net to meet them, defeated. She forced a smile on her sweat-drenched face, clasping first Claudia's hand, then T.J.'s in the traditional loser to winner salute. Don did the same.

"I'll never understand why you didn't try out for the tennis team," Cassie said to her sister. "You're almost as good as I am—better in some ways."

Claudia shrugged. "It interfered with my dance classes. But you're much better than I am, Cass. It was sheer luck that you couldn't reach that ball. I've never been very good at placement."

Cassie, the pockets of her white shorts still bulging with tennis balls, laughed and said, "You placed that shot perfectly, and don't tell me you didn't plan it that way!"

"Well, I *tried*," Claudia admitted coyly. "And for once, it worked. Hey, I'm so thirsty I could drink up the entire lake! Let's get some sodas, OK?"

The four friends walked up to the wide porch of the club's main building, T.J.'s arm around Claudia and Don's around Cassie.

They kept rehashing points of the game in a friendly fashion as they drank their soda, until at last T.J. said, "How about making a day of it? We could have lunch here, then go to the amusement park and celebrate."

"Yeah, celebrate your victory and our defeat," said Cassie with a mock scowl. "But it sounds like a great idea. What do you say, Claude?"

Claudia nodded happily. "I'd love it!"

"Let's have a swim first," Don suggested. "You brought your suits, didn't you?" he asked the girls.

"We're never around Green Lake without them," Cassie said.

"I'll show you where the women's locker room is, then T.J. and I will meet you down by the water, OK?"

A few minutes later, Cassie and Claudia had taken their things into the locker room and were busy changing from sweat-soaked tennis clothes into swimsuits.

"I can't get over what a good tennis player Don is," said Cassie, struggling into her suit. "It wasn't his fault that we lost, it was mine. Maybe I was trying too hard."

"You were both great," Claudia said. "And T.J. is so much better than I am that he made us both look good. Did you notice that serve of his? Jimmy Connors, eat your heart out!"

"*Notice* it? I could hardly see it!" wailed Cassie. "Whenever he was serving to me, I just kind of closed my eyes and prayed."

"But you returned everything," Claudia reminded her.

"Yeah, most of the time right into the net! You and T.J. make a good team. You're good at the net, and he's fantastic with baseline rallies." Cassie pulled the sweatband from around her head. "Look at my hair. I look like a drowned rat!"

"Just fluff it up a little," Claudia advised. "It'll be even wetter when we start to swim."

"I shouldn't have cut it. If I'd kept it long, like yours, it would be OK."

"Well, don't say I didn't warn you," Claudia said smugly, then hastily added, "But it doesn't really look bad. The guys won't notice your hair when they see your figure in that suit!"

"Oh, come on!" Cassie groaned. "Next to you, I look more like an elephant!" But she had to admit, appraising her image in the mirror, that her figure *was* pretty good. She was curvaceous and womanly. Claudia, on the other hand, was as slender as a reed in her

turquoise bikini. Which would appeal more to
T.J.? she wondered. For the first time, she
thought about being in competition with her
twin for a boy's attention, and it made her
uncomfortable. They'd never been rivals
before. But then, they'd never been interested
in the same boy. And now, Cassie realized
with a pang, they were.

"Ready?" asked Claudia, slipping her feet
into rubber thong sandals.

"Ready when you are," Cassie replied, running her fingers through her tousled hair.
"Let's not keep the guys waiting." But she
knew that neither of them was concerned with
Don's reaction, only T.J.'s, and the knowledge
was not particularly pleasant.

"Boy, you two took long enough," said Don
as the two girls crossed the grassy strip that
separated the club building from the water.
"Not that it wasn't worth it," he added admiringly.

"Race you to the dock!" shouted Cassie,
dashing for the cool, sparkling water. She surface dived and struck out for the floating dock
that was connected by a rope and bright-
colored buoys to the shore. She reached the
dock seconds before any of the others and

pulled herself onto its sun-hot surface, laughing down at T.J., who was the next to arrive.

"Beatcha!" she cried as he scrambled up beside her.

"No fair! You had a head start!"

He climbed onto the dock and flung himself down next to Cassie, shaking a shower of diamond-bright droplets from his hair like a wet dog. Cassie admired his tanned, muscular body glistening in the midday sun. Claudia and Don were still frolicking in the water, making no effort to join them. She saw Claudia's head surface, then disappear as she dived down once again, Don laughing at her side.

I ought to say something, Cassie thought, for the first time at a loss for words. It suddenly seemed very important that she be interesting and amusing. "You and Don are going to college this fall, right?" she said finally. *Boring, Cass!* she told herself, but it was the first thing that popped into her head.

"Yeah, we're both going to Gettysburg. Is that anywhere near where you live?"

Delighted, Cassie sat up. "It's only about twenty-five miles away! Gettysburg? Really? That's great!"

"It sure is. Small world, huh?"

"So maybe we'll see you—both of you—sometime," she said hopefully.

"Wait till I tell Don! It'll blow his mind! Don told me he really likes you a lot, Cassie. Like I said, he's kind of shy around girls, but he's a great guy—lots of fun." T.J. rolled over onto his back, arms folded beneath his head as he gazed up at Cassie.

Cassie looked away, concentrating on a piece of the dock's canvas covering that had torn away from the wood beneath.

"I kind of got the impression he was interested in Claudia," she murmured, glancing up at the two of them in the water, both floating on their backs side by side.

"Maybe that's because Claudia's kind of—quiet. Not threatening, you know? Not that you are," T.J. added hastily. "Don's always gone for the outgoing type, like you. But the girls he likes are usually hung up on some dumb jock type. They don't appreciate his good qualities."

The conversation was getting too heavy for Cassie's enjoyment. She turned away from T.J. and shouted, "Hey, you guys! Aren't you ever going to come out of the water? You'll wrinkle up like prunes."

Claudia and Don waved and made for the

dock. Don pulled himself out of the water and flopped down beside Cassie. Claudia ended up sitting next to T.J. She was smiling a lot, and she didn't bother to conceal her braces, Cassie noted. After a while, the sun warmed them up again, and all four plunged back into the lake, heading for the shore.

"Let's get dressed and have lunch at the snack bar," T.J. suggested. "They have really good hot dogs. Then we'll take off for Herman's."

"Who's Herman?" asked Claudia.

"Not who, what. That's the amusement park in Fennimore," Don said.

"Oh, we passed by it the other day, but I didn't notice the name," said Cassie. "We'll met you at the snack bar."

The hot dogs were, as T.J. had promised, delicious. Both girls ate two, complete with mustard, relish, and onions, and washed them down with lots of soda. When they were all full to bursting, they piled into T.J.'s old Rabbit, Don and T.J. in the front and Claudia and Cassie in the rear.

"I know it's not exactly luxurious back there," T.J. apologized, "but you two have shorter legs, so you won't be quite as uncomfortable as Don would be, with his knees up against his chin."

With two hot dogs and all that soda creating a turmoil in her stomach, Claudia actually did feel pretty uncomfortable, but she didn't want to mention it. Once they reached Herman's, she thought, she'd be able to stretch her legs—and her stomach.

T.J. pulled into the rutted parking lot a few minutes later, and they all got out, much to Claudia's relief. Cassie looked as though she was happy to be through with the jolting, bouncing ride, too. The boys immediately headed for a shooting gallery. They both won wildly colored stuffed animals, which they gave to the girls—a brilliant blue bear for Cassie and a magenta cat for Claudia. The next stop was the Tilt-A-Whirl. Cassie screamed in delight, but Claudia didn't feel all that great when they got off. She suggested the Ferris wheel, which had a lovely view of Fennimore Lake from the top. Sharing a seat with T.J. was awfully nice, too.

Next came the merry-go-round. Cassie rode a zebra with an intricate real leather bridle while Claudia chose a dapple-gray steed whose saddle was decorated with fake gems.

84

Then came Italian sausage sandwiches, more soda, and cotton candy.

"Let's ride the swings," cried Cassie, pointing to a ride on which individual swing seats hung by long chains and circled around a gigantic central post.

Claudia, by now feeling queasy, wanted to pass, but the others urged her on. "Come on, Claudia, it'll be fun," said Don. Not wanting to put a damper on the afternoon, Claudia reluctantly agreed. But the moment the swings began to fly around, she knew it had been a major error. Everything she'd eaten over the past few hours seemed to be churning inside her, creating waves of nausea that she couldn't overcome no matter how hard she tried. She managed to grit her teeth for the length of the ride, which seemed to last an eternity, but as soon as her feet hit solid ground, she clutched Cassie's arm, and whispered, "I'm going to be sick!"

"Oh, no!" wailed Cassie, looking frantically around for a secluded spot.

But it was too late. Claudia doubled over and deposited the remains of the hot dogs, soda, sausages, and cotton candy on the ground right by the ticket booth. She was dimly conscious of a firm hand on her elbow.

"It's OK," came T.J.'s voice through her misery. "Don't worry about it. Would you like some ginger ale? That always helps me when I get sick."

"OK, whatever . . ." Claudia mumbled, sick at heart as well as at stomach. "I'm sorry."

"Nothing to worry about," T.J. said gently. "Don, want to get Claudia a ginger ale?" As Don hurried off to the nearest stand, T.J. maintained his grip on Claudia's arm. "We'll take you home, all right? I guess we kind of overdid it with the heat and all. You can ride in front. Not that it's much better than riding in the back, in my car, but it's the best I can do."

"OK. I'm fine now, really I am," Claudia whispered. Her mouth tasted terrible. Turning to her sister, she said, "Cass, I'm sorry. I have this funny stomach . . ."

"If anybody should know about your funny stomach, it's me," Cassie soothed, stroking Claudia's damp forehead. "Don'll be back in a second with the ginger ale, and we'll go home. Don't worry."

The ride home seemed endless to both Claudia and Cassie. Claudia still felt nauseated, and Cassie felt responsible for her twin's well-being. When at last T.J. stopped the car in front of their cabin, Claudia crawled out, her face a sickly green, quickly followed by Cassie, who said, "Thanks for everything, T.J., Don. Claudia'll be fine. She's always had a weak stomach. No big deal."

"I'll call you tonight," T.J. offered, "to see how she is. Maybe I ought to come in and explain to your parents . . ."

"No, please. I'll be OK after I lie down for a while," said Claudia with as much confidence as she could muster. "Thanks, both of you, for a really wonderful day."

"Yeah—wonderful," Don echoed, his voice uncertain. "You're sure? . . ."

"Sure," Claudia mumbled, making for the door. She felt totally drained and as weak as a kitten. All she wanted to do was collapse on her bunk and get over the hideous nausea that still held her in its grip, not to mention the even more hideous embarrassment.

"I'll call tonight," repeated T.J. as he drove away.

Claudia wished she could crawl into a corner and die. She was glad that their parents were out on some expedition or other so she didn't have to explain what a fool she'd made of herself.

"I'm really sorry, Cass," she said wearily as she started up the stairs to their room. "I ruined the day for all of us. It's just that everything kind of—oh, I don't know! I *hate* it when something like this happens! We were having such fun. . . ."

"Hey, Claude, shut up, OK? No big deal. I'm sure both T.J. and Don have seen people throw up before. They're not going to stop being friends with us because of this," Cassie said, following her sister up the steps.

Claudia flopped down on her bunk, burying her face in the pillow. "Thanks, Cass. I think I'd like to sleep for a while. If T.J. really does call . . ."

". . . you'll be all recovered and you'll talk to him yourself," said Cassie firmly. "Take a nap now. Do you want anything?"

"No, I just want to sleep. See you later." She sighed deeply.

Cassie went back downstairs, her feet dragging. What if Claudia's illness *had* turned the boys off completely? she thought. Well, if so, they weren't worth worrying about, were they?

Chapter Seven

Claudia ate very little at dinner that night. Though her stomach was back to normal, she couldn't help thinking about what a fool she'd made of herself at Herman's. And not just a fool, a *disgusting* fool, she thought. T.J. had been polite, but he must have been really grossed out.

"No salad, Claudia?" asked her mother. Claudia shook her head, and her mother asked, "Aren't you feeling well, dear?"

"I'm all right," Claudia said and sighed.

"She got sick on the rides at the amusement park this afternoon and threw up all over T.J.," Cassie put in cheerfully.

"Oh, Cass, I did *not* throw up all over him! Don't make it sound worse than it was. It was bad enough."

"That's a shame," Mr. Fletcher said sympathetically, then grinned slyly at his wife. "Brings back fond memories, doesn't it, Lydia?"

Mrs. Fletcher laughed ruefully. "Not exactly fond, but I know what you're talking about."

"We don't. Fill us in," Cassie urged.

"Well, the first time I went on a real date with your father, I wanted to impress him with how sophisticated I was," Mrs. Fletcher began. "He took me to a very elegant restaurant—"

"I wanted to impress *her* with how sophisticated *I* was," Mr. Fletcher cut in.

"Anyway, the first course was raw clams. He'd ordered them for me, told me I'd love them. Little did he know! I managed to swallow two of the slimy little things, feeling sicker by the minute."

"She turned an alarming shade of green," added Mr. Fletcher.

"*Anyway,*" said Mrs. Fletcher, glaring at her husband, "I took one look at the third clam, and that did it. I knew I was about to disgrace myself. So I jumped up, knocked over my chair, and dashed down the hall, heading for what I thought was the door to the ladies' room. Unfortunately, it turned out to be some kind of supply closet. I threw up all over the brooms and mops, not to mention my best dress and brand new shoes. Talk about sophistication. I thought I'd die!"

"Poor Mom! How gross!" Claudia laughed.

"What about poor Dad?" Mr. Fletcher asked. "I had to sneak out the back door and take her right home. All my dreams of a romantic evening went up in smoke."

"But you married her anyway," Cassie pointed out. "Fortunately for us!"

Suddenly Claudia felt a lot better and even ate some pound cake and ice cream for dessert.

A few hours later, the Fletchers were seated around the card table, in the midst of the long-delayed game of Parcheesi, when the telephone rang. *Could it be T.J.?* Claudia wondered. *He said he'd call.* Not wanting to seem eager, she said casually to her twin, "Cass, why don't you get it?"

But Cassie was already at the phone, picking up the receiver. Claudia strained her ears to catch Cassie's end of the conversation.

"Hello? . . . No, it's Cassie. Hi, T.J. . . . Oh, she's fine. All better. . . . OK, I will. . . . Oh, that'd be terrific! I'm sure she'd love to. Seven o'clock? Great? See you both then!"

"That was T.J.," she said unnecessarily, coming back to the table. "He wanted to know how you were feeling, Claude, and then he asked if we'd like to go to the movies with him and Don tomorrow night. There's a rerun of *Return of the Jedi* playing in Andersville. They'll pick us up around seven. I said OK. I figured you wouldn't have any objections, right?"

"Sure, why not?" said Claudia, joy flooding through her. T.J. couldn't have been too disgusted if he wanted to take them out again. "Is it all right with you?" she asked their parents, who smiled and nodded their assent.

"Those are two very nice young men," said Mr. Fletcher. "And your mother and I are playing bridge with the Howards tomorrow night, so we'll be occupied. . . . Cassie, I hate to do this to my very own child, but here goes!" His man landed on one of Cassie's, sending it back home.

"Rats!" Cassie groaned. "And I was more than halfway around the board! Have you no pity?"

"None," said her father smugly. "Your turn, Lydia. You may be the checker champ, but Fearless Frank is the undisputed prince of Parcheesi!"

*   *   *

Promptly at seven the following evening, Claudia and Cassie heard a car pull up. Running to the window, Claudia said, "It's T.J. and Don, all right, but they're in a different car, and Don's driving."

Cassie joined her, peering over her shoulder. "Thank goodness! I wasn't exactly looking forward to being stuck in the back of T.J.'s Rabbit again." Then she made a face. "Gee, I hope Don's not as clumsy behind the wheel of a car as he is on foot, or we'll end up in a ditch!"

She went to open the door at T.J.'s knock, smiling into his sparkling eyes. "Hi. Want to come in for a minute while Claude and I get our things?"

"No, that's OK, I'll wait in the car. It's Don's father's. We thought we'd spare you the pretzel treatment tonight," said T.J. "Take your time. The movie doesn't start until seven forty-five." T.J. went back to the car.

"Claude, where are you? Come on!" Cassie called to her twin as she searched in the closet for her light summer jacket. She found it and draped it over her shoulders, checking her appearance in the little mirror by the door. She was glad she'd decided to wear her red-

and-white striped rubgy shirt with her white jeans, particularly since T.J. was wearing an almost identical shirt, only in blue and white. She ran her fingers through her hair, fluffing it around her face a little, as Claudia came down the stairs.

Cassie was amused to see that her sister had changed her blouse at the last minute. Instead of the pale blue, man-tailored shirt she'd been wearing, she now had on a pink flowered blouse, and her ponytail was tied with a matching pink ribbon. Her cheeks were pink, too.

"Changed my mind," Claudia said airily in answer to Cassie's raised eyebrows. She snatched a white sweater from the arm of a chair. "Come on, slowpoke! What are we waiting for?"

"Rugby shirts to the rear," called Don. T.J. opened the car door, and Cassie slid in beside him. Claudia sat next to Don in the front.

T.J. leaned over the seat, saying to Claudia, "You're really OK? I mean, you look great. You both look great. But you're feeling all right?"

"Absolutely!" said Claudia over her shoulder. "No revolting behavior tonight, I promise."

"We're not that easily revolted," said Don as

he started the car. "*Return of the Jedi* here we come!" He reached down and turned on the cassette player, flooding the car with the sound of Van Halen's latest album, and so the conversation during the drive into town was carried on at top volume over the music.

Claudia was very conscious of T.J.'s presence directly behind her. She wondered whose idea the seating arrangement had been. Had T.J. told Don he wanted to sit with Cassie? Or had Don decided he wanted Claudia to sit with him? *Don't be dumb*, she told herself sternly. *We're not really couples, just four people going out to have a good time.* Seated happily next to T.J., Cassie was thinking that whoever had made the choice, it had worked out very well indeed.

During the movie, Cassie sat between Don and T.J., while Claudia sat on T.J.'s other side, very much aware of the warmth of his arm lightly touching hers. Afterward, as they ambled down the street to the ice cream parlor, Don and a sniffling Cassie led the way, with T.J. and Claudia, also teary-eyed, at their heels.

"I thought you said you'd seen the movie before," said T.J. as Claudia blew her nose.

"We have, twice. And we cry at the end every time," Claudia admitted.

"I got a little choked up myself," T.J. said and grinned, which made Claudia feel better.

Just then Don tripped over a crack in the sidewalk, and Cassie grabbed his arm to keep him from falling. He promptly tucked her arm in his. "For security," he joked. T.J. reached out and took Claudia's hand. It was as though little shivers of electricity zipped right up her arm, and she knew she was blushing. She was glad it was dark out so no one could see her overreaction to T.J.'s gesture. He was just being friendly. But the electric tingle continued all the way to the ice cream parlor.

Don had recommended Sweet's enthusiastically, saying it had the best homemade ice cream in all of New York State.

When they arrived, they were joined by a group of T.J. and Don's friends, most of whom had seen *Return of the Jedi*. Everybody was talking loudly about the movie and exchanging local gossip. Cassie and Claudia found themselves squeezed into a booth with Don, T.J., Pat from the Green Lake store, and her boyfriend, Larry. It was all very cozy, though a little cramped, and the ice cream was, true to Don's description, creamy and thick. Claudia was content to enjoy hers in silence while she listened to Cassie's hot debate with the boys about the merits and faults of various tennis players.

The argument continued between Cassie and T.J. as the group left the ice cream parlor. It had turned into a heated discussion of the skills and stamina of men versus women on the courts. T.J. said it was obvious that women were still the weaker sex since they were only required to play three sets in a match, whereas men played five. "I'm with Bobby Riggs. When he challenged Billie Jean King to a match, he said any man could beat any woman."

"And she won!" shouted Cassie triumphantly. "So much for male chauvinism!"

"Yeah, well, she was younger, in better physical shape, and a much better player than he was," T.J. admitted with a smile. "But it's the principle of the thing that counts."

Cassie wasn't convinced one bit. "That's absolutely, totally, completely illogical! I'll tell you what, *I* challenge *you* to a match! One on one, five sets. I'm only about a year younger than you, so age isn't a factor. We're both in pretty good shape. And it may sound conceited, but I think I'm probably as good a player as you are!"

"You're on! When do you want to do it?"

"When's your next day off?" Cassie snapped.

Claudia and Don's heads swiveled back and forth from one to the other as though the tennis match were already in progress.

"The store's closed on Sundays, but I'm busy tomorrow. I have Tuesday off next week, though. How about ten o'clock, at the club?" T.J. was grinning broadly, as though certain of his upcoming victory.

"Shake!" said Cassie, sticking out her right hand. T.J. took it and pumped it firmly. Then laughing, he put his arm around her shoulders as they walked to the car.

"Hey, I'm going to start taking bets," Don said. "Who're you going to put your money on, Claudia?"

"Blood is thicker than water," Claudia responded virtuously, then thought a moment and said, "Fifty cents on T.J.!"

"Traitor!" Cassie cried. "You'd think my own *sister* would have faith in me!"

"I have faith in you both," Claudia said, grinning impishly. "But in this case, I have *more* faith in T.J."

"That's what I like to hear!" said T.J., putting his other arm around Claudia and giving her a quick hug.

"No fair! Let me in on this," said Don, putting his arm around Cassie's waist from the other side. Laughing, they walked four abreast down the sidewalk. Secretly, both twins' hearts were singing.

"I've got to be out of my mind!" Cassie said later that night as the girls got ready for bed. "Whatever made me challenge T.J. to a five-set match? Why didn't you stop me?"

"Would you have listened if I'd tried?" Claudia asked dryly, crawling into her bunk.

Cassie sighed. "Probably not. If I lose, he'll think I'm just a weakling with a big mouth. I've got to win!"

"I'm sure he wouldn't think that at all," said Claudia. "But he's a very good tennis player. He'll probably cream you. You never know, though. Maybe he'll give you a loser's hug instead of the usual handshake."

"Yuk!" Cassie said. "Not that I'd mind a hug from T.J., but not under those circumstances." Then she burst out, "Oh, Claudia, he's the most wonderful boy I've ever met! I really think I'm falling in love with him!" She perched on the edge of her sister's bunk. "Claude, tell me the truth. Do you think he's starting to like me a little?"

"Of course he likes you." Claudia avoided Cassie's gaze, afraid that her own feelings would show too plainly. "But if you're asking if he's falling in love with you, I can't answer that. Why don't you ask *him*?"

"Oh, sure. Big help you are."

Cassie swung up into her bunk and lay on her back, arms folded under her head. She was staring at the ceiling, but instead of knotty pine boards, she saw T.J.'s face. She could hear the sound of his deep, teasing voice, feel his arm around her . . .

"Aren't you going to write in your diary, Cass?" Claudia called, interrupting her fantasy. "You didn't take it out of the drawer."

"What? Oh, I almost forgot." T.J.'s image remained in Cassie's mind as she asked dreamily, "Would you hand it to me, please?"

Sighing, Claudia got out of bed, padded to the bureau, fished out the diary, and handed it up to her sister. "Tell me when you're through and I'll turn out the light," she said.

Cassie wrote for a long time, describing their evening in detail. Whenever she came to T.J.'s name, she doodled a little heart around the two initials, knowing it was silly but taking pleasure in it just the same. When she had finished, she reread what she'd written, smiling to herself, then added a few more sentences.

I was kidding when I wrote before that I was falling madly in love with T.J., but now I think I really am. I asked Claude just now if she thought maybe he was beginning to feel the same way, and she told me to ask him. Fat chance!

Suddenly Cassie's eyes widened as a new thought struck her. She wrote the final sentence very slowly: "I wonder if maybe she's falling in love with him herself."

She closed the diary and was about to pass it down over the side for Claudia's comments, then changed her mind. "OK, you can turn out the light now," she said softly.

Claudia didn't ask to read her entry, just got out of bed and flicked the switch. "Night, Cass," she said, getting back into bed.

"Night, Claude."

But that's crazy, Cassie said to herself as she lay in her bunk, wide awake. *She'd tell me if she felt that way—wouldn't she? Sure she would! Maybe I ought to ask her.*

"Claude?"

"What?"

"Listen, about T.J. . . ."

"Hmm?"

No, I won't ask her. We don't keep secrets from each other. She'd let me know if there was anything to tell, Cassie thought. "I'm going to have to practice like crazy for that tennis match," she said instead. "Will you come to the club with me tomorrow and hit a few balls around?"

"Sure. Tomorrow morning?"

"Yeah, right after breakfast. Thanks, Claude."

So Cassie's falling in love with him, too. Claudia stared out the half-opened balcony door at the moon-drenched sky, her thoughts churning. *Oh, why couldn't she fall in love with Don instead? Or why couldn't I?*

Chapter Eight

The next morning dawned gray. It was the first day since the Fletchers had arrived at Green Lake that there hadn't been brilliant sunshine. Cassie immediately tuned in a local radio station during breakfast and learned that scattered showers were predicted for later that day.

"Come on, Claude, let's get moving," she said as soon as the breakfast dishes were washed. They walked into the living room, where their parents were sitting, having more coffee. "Daddy, will you drive us to the club? It's only a mile past the store. Claude and I have to play tennis this morning."

"Have to?" asked Mrs. Fletcher, setting down her cup.

"Absolutely! I have a big match coming up on Tuesday," said Cassie. "Why don't you come along, Mom? You've never been to the club. Maybe you and Daddy could play, too."

"What big match? I seem to be a couple of beats behind you," said Mr. Fletcher. "What's happening? Fill me in, please."

"Cass challenged T.J. to a five-set match last night," Claudia shouted from the hallway, where she took two rackets and two cans of balls out of the closet. "They got into a big argument about men and women, and Cassie said he was crazy, so they're playing Tuesday morning to see who's right. Cass wants to get in a lot of practice between now and then."

"My goodness!" said Mrs. Fletcher. "Your father and I are going to an antiques auction this afternoon, but it might be fun to stretch the old muscles a little and play some tennis before it starts to rain. What do you think, Frank?"

Mr. Fletcher shrugged. "Why not? We'll change into our tennis clothes and meet you at the car in about ten minutes."

"Make that fifteen," amended Mrs. Fletcher. "I'm not exactly sure where I put my tennis shorts."

"Daddy used to be pretty good," Claudia

said to her twin as they waited for their parents to come downstairs. "Maybe you ought to hit some balls with him."

"That's a good idea. He has a dynamite serve. It would really keep me on my toes."

Cassie was practicing shots against a phantom opponent with her racket still in its press. "Wow, that really strains my arm!"

"You'll do fine," Claudia encouraged. "You may not win, but you'll give T.J. a good workout."

"Boy, you're a real confidence booster, you know that?" said Cassie sarcastically. "I suppose it never occurred to you that I just might win?"

"Cass, you said yourself last night you didn't think you could beat him."

"Well, things look better in the light of day. Don't we have a couple of cans of new balls?"

"Got 'em," said Claudia, pointing toward a chest in the hallway. "Want your warm-up jacket? It's a little chilly."

"OK. Maybe the pants, too." Cassie sneezed. "Darn! I hope I'm not getting a cold."

"It's probably just an allergy. The radio said there was a very high pollen count today."

"Oh, wonderful, just what I need. I'll get ready to serve, and I'll have a sneezing fit."

Cassie went to the foot of the stairs. "Mom? Dad? Are you about ready?"

"Coming," called Mrs. Fletcher.

"Mom, could you get Cassie's warm-up suit from our room? She wants it," Claudia called up.

A few minutes later, all four Fletchers were heading for the club under increasingly cloudy skies.

"This is it," said Cassie, pointing out a partially concealed driveway. "Just tell them we're renting the Fergusons' cabin, and it'll be OK."

There weren't many people at the club that morning. The regulars had apparently stayed home, put off by the threatening weather, so there was no waiting list for the tennis courts. Mr. and Mrs. Fletcher began warming up on the court next to the one Claudia and Cassie had chosen.

Claudia opened a second can of balls, stood up, and swung her arms a few times. "OK, champ, here we go!" she cried, serving accurately into Cassie's court.

After a few practice shots, Cassie stripped out of her warm-up suit and began playing her hardest. She kept her eye on the ball, returning Claudia's shots. When it was her turn to serve, she put every ounce of strength behind

106

her racket. Claudia had a hard time sending the balls back over the net.

"Hey, cool it, Navratilova!" she shouted, after lunging for a particularly well-placed shot. "You're not playing Tracy Austin or some other pro, you know!"

"I'm pretending I'm John McEnroe and you're Jimmy Connors. It helps," Cassie yelled back, sending the ball in a high forehand lob right into the far corner of Claudia's court. Claudia leaped for it and missed.

"Good shot!" she called. "T.J.'s going to have to run his legs off if you keep this up!"

"That's what I have in mind," Cassie admitted. "I figure if I can wear him out running back and forth, he'll have less energy to put into the rest of his game."

"Sneaky, sneaky!" Claudia laughed. "It's certainly working with me. But then, I'm only a poor, weak *girl*!"

After about an hour, Claudia took on her mother while Cassie confronted Mr. Fletcher. He'd been a champion a few years before at the tennis club in their hometown, and now he called on all his strength and agility to keep his daughter hopping. Every so often they'd stop, and he'd give her pointers on her form and footwork.

By noon a light rain had begun to fall, and everyone but Cassie was ready to call it a day. Cassie would have played on in a downpour, but the girls' parents were firm.

"Tomorrow morning again, OK?" she asked eagerly as they slogged through the wet grass toward the parking lot.

Mr. Fletcher grimaced. "If I'm not a basket case by then and if the rain lets up. I haven't had so much exercise in years. I'm going to need a vacation to recuperate from my vacation!"

"It'll all be over by Tuesday," Cassie reassured him. "Boy, wouldn't it be great if I really *did* beat him?"

"I thought you were nuts about him," said Claudia. "You sound as though you want to slaughter him."

Cassie laughed. "All's fair in love and war, and this is *war*! But it doesn't mean that I'm mad at him or anything."

"When I was a girl," Mrs. Fletcher put in primly, "if you liked a boy, you got all dressed up in your prettiest dress and hung around looking sweet and feminine. You might even tell the boy what a big, strong, wonderful guy he was." She sighed. "Things have certainly changed."

"Oh, Mom," cried Cassie, "you sound as though you grew up in the Dark Ages! What's really important is for a girl and boy to have something in common and to respect each other's abilities. I mean, that's the way it should be."

Cassie's right, Claudia thought, suddenly depressed. Her sister and T.J. were two of a kind, outgoing, sports-minded, competitive. She, on the other hand, was none of those things. What could T.J. ever see in her? She sighed to herself, thinking, *Cassie and T.J. are made for each other, and there's absolutely nothing I can do about it.*

"What's the matter?" asked Cassie.

Claudia shrugged. "Just tired, I guess. It looks like today is going to be perfect for curling up with a good book, which is about all I'm up to right now."

"I'm with you. I think I really *am* getting a cold. My throat feels scratchy."

"Have you been taking your vitamin C?" asked Mrs. Fletcher. When Cassie admitted that she hadn't, her mother made her promise to take some as soon as they got back to the cabin.

"I'll take half the bottle if it'll keep me from getting a cold," said Cassie, rubbing her throat. "I absolutely, positively *refuse* to be feeling less than super-perfect for the big match!"

Just as they reached the car, the downpour started. Quickly they got inside. Claudia slid down in her seat, looking out at the rain, which was now streaming down the windows. *The big match—a match made in heaven*, she thought, and her spirits sank even lower.

In spite of vitamin C and endless cups of hot tea with honey and lemon, it was apparent within a couple of hours that Cassie had developed a cold, complete with sneezing, stuffy nose, and sore throat. Added to that, the rain had settled into a steady downpour, and everything inside the cabin as well as outside was clammy and damp. Mr. Fletcher built a roaring fire in the wood stove to take some of the chill out of the air. Then he and Mrs. Fletcher took off for their auction, swathed in rain gear. Cassie sat next to the stove wrapped up in a blanket, trying to concentrate on an old novel she'd found on the Fergusons' bookshelves. But the pages were mildewed and stuck together, and at last she tossed it aside, wailing, "It's not fair! I won't be able to practice tomorrow if this blasted rain doesn't let up! And what if it rains on Tuesday? Oh, rats!"

"Well, T.J. won't be able to practice either, so you'll be even. And if it does rain, you'll just postpone the match," Claudia pointed out, looking up from *Jane Eyre*. "Besides, it really wouldn't be fair if you'd been practicing like mad and T.J. couldn't because he was working. Anyway, the weather report says the rain's supposed to stop by tomorrow afternoon. If you're feeling OK, you'll be able to play."

"I'm going to play no matter what," said Cassie, reaching for another tissue and blowing her nose. "But my nose will be red as a beet, and I'll look terrible!"

True, Claudia thought, and was horrified and ashamed to realize that the thought pleased her. *What's happening to me?* she wondered unhappily. *Cassie's my best friend as well as my sister. I shouldn't be happy that she's feeling lousy and looks bad.* To make up for her disloyalty, she suggested, "Why don't you take a nap? You'll feel better after you've rested for a while."

Cassie struggled to her feet. "I might as well." She moaned. "I couldn't feel worse!"

By the end of the following day, the rain had

stopped. Despite her streaming nose, Cassie wandered around the cabin, swinging her racket at invisible balls and sneezing unhappily.

"Cassie, maybe you'd better call T.J. and reschedule the match," suggested her mother.

"No way!" cried Cassie. "It'll look like I'm copping out, like I'm using my cold as an excuse. I'll play if it kills me!"

"Don't be so stubborn, Cass," Claudia urged. "You can't play your best when you're feeling rotten, and T.J. certainly wouldn't want to take advantage of your illness. Why don't you call him?"

"Forget it, Claude," said her sister firmly. "*He* wouldn't back out if he wasn't feeling well, and neither will I." She sneezed again. "It's simply mind over matter. Tomorrow I'm going to be feeling *terrific*!"

The next morning, the sun was shining brightly. The mist that had shrouded the lake for the past two days had lifted at last, and the water sparkled. Cassie wasn't feeling exactly terrific, but her cold was a little better. *It's wonderful,* she mused as she dressed, *how nice weather can raise your spirits.* She looked at herself anxiously in the mirror, wondering if the redness of her nose was terribly apparent. Thanks to her tan, it was hardly noticeable. And she looked positively slim and trim in her clean white shorts and shirt—maybe not as slim as Claudia, but certainly not pudgy.

By nine o'clock she had eaten a light breakfast and was eager to get to the courts and limber up before T.J. arrived. She was practicing her two-handed backhand while waiting impatiently for Claudia and her parents to get themselves together and drive to the club, when Mr. Fletcher joined her on the deck.

"Cassie, your mother and I have been discussing this match—" he began.

"Oh, Daddy, you're not going to tell me I can't play!" cried Cassie.

"Nothing so world-shaking as that. But we've agreed that it's crazy to go five sets. Even if you were in the best of health, it would be grueling. Three sets will be quite enough to prove your point."

"But, Daddy! The point is that women have as much endurance as men! If I play only three sets, T.J. will think it's because I can't handle five. And I know I can!"

"Cassie, we've made our decision. It's three sets or none at all," said her mother in a tone of voice that meant she would not be budged.

Cassie looked from her father to her mother, then glanced at Claudia, who just shrugged helplessly.

"I'll tell T.J. if you like," Mr. Fletcher suggested.

Cassie scowled and swiped her racket in what would have been a lethal forehand drive if there had been a ball to hit. "No, I'll tell him myself," she mumbled angrily. "Would it be *too* much to ask for everybody to get moving? It's a quarter after nine. At least you can let me warm up, for goodness' sake!"

The drive to the club was made in gloomy silence. Cassie slumped in a corner in the backseat staring bleakly out the window. Claudia's attempts at conversation were met with brief replies, so she gave up. Why was it so important to Cassie to prove that she was T.J.'s equal in sports? she wondered. She guessed it was just Cassie's competitive drive, a drive she'd never really shared, although she knew that if a male dancer assumed men could dance longer and better than women just because they were men, she'd be absolutely furious.

"Hey, Cass, your new tennis shorts look really great," she said at last. "I think you've lost weight this past week."

Cassie flashed her a grateful look, the first Claudia had seen of the cheerful old Cassie since they'd left the house.

"I haven't eaten a Twinkie in four whole days," Cassie confided, and then they both giggled, the harmony between them restored for the moment.

Claudia and Cassie were volleying when T.J. and Don came ambling across the grass toward the courts, accompanied by several of their friends.

"Oh, good grief!" said Cassie. "I wasn't counting on an audience."

T.J. dropped his warm-up jacket on a bench and marched over to Cassie, waving at Claudia as he passed. "Cassie, I have something to tell you," he said a little sheepishly.

"What?" she asked, realizing that it had to be pretty important. She'd never seen T.J. look so serious.

"Listen, I don't want you to think that I'm copping out or anything, but, well, I stepped on a piece of glass yesterday, and I cut the sole of my foot pretty badly. I'm going to play," he hastily assured her when he saw her dismayed expression, "but I'm not going to be able to play five sets. If you'll agree to three, we're still on."

"Oh, that's great!" Cassie cried. Then, realizing that her enthusiasm might be misunderstood, she added, "I'm sorry you hurt yourself—"

"Yeah, sounds like something *I* would do, right?" Don put in and grinned.

"—but my mother and dad just told me that they didn't want me to play five sets, either, because I've had this rotten cold. So I guess it's fate or something," she finished, beaming.

"Hey, come on, you guys!" shouted one of the boys. "We came out here for a tennis match, and so far all you two have done is talk!"

"Let's do it," said T.J., going over to the opposite side of the court just as Claudia was leaving it.

"Are you sure your foot's all right? It doesn't hurt or anything?" she asked anxiously.

He looked down at her with a smile that made her knees go weak. "I'm fine. I had a tetanus shot and everything. No sweat."

"OK. I was worried," Claudia said. "And good luck. I have fifty cents riding on this match, you know!"

T.J. grinned and took a tennis ball out of

the pocket of his shorts. "Hey, Cassie, coming at you!" he called and served the first ball as Claudia dodged out of the way.

T.J. won the first set 6—4, and Cassie took the second by a narrow margin, in spite of the hacking cough that occasionally bothered her. As they began the third and final set, Claudia felt the tension building inside her. She was torn between rooting for her sister and rooting for T.J., so she applauded every good shot, not caring which one of them had hit it. She thought T.J. was beginning to look a little strained, as though the cut on his foot was bothering him more than he liked to admit. As for Cassie, though she kept sneezing and blowing her nose, she seemed to be holding up pretty well.

"Hang in there, Cassie," her father muttered, completely absorbed in the match. "On your toes . . . watch that backhand . . . don't rush the net. . . ." The other onlookers, quite a crop by now, were fairly evenly divided between T.J., cheered by most of the boys, and Cassie, whom the girls favored. Don, the scorekeeper, was impassive, though Claudia suspected he was on T.J.'s side.

At last they reached the deciding point. Cassie, standing ready to receive T.J.'s serve, felt sweat dampen the palms of her hands as she clutched her racket. *It's now or never*, she thought, her eyes riveted on T.J. behind the baseline. Suddenly the sunlight caught his wavy hair, turning it into a golden aureole around his head, and she felt a catch at her throat that was not due to her cold. *What am I doing?* she asked herself, momentarily distracted. *I love him. I don't want to beat him!* But then her spirit of competition took over, and she tossed her head as though to clear it of all other thoughts. Bouncing lightly on the balls of her feet, she glued her gaze to T.J.'s racket as it made contact with the ball.

The ball whizzed over the net, and she returned it with all the power at her command. T.J. sped across the court, then winced and faltered. His return, which would have placed the ball in center court if he'd been in complete control, barely grazed the top of the net. The ball limped over and landed just beyond Cassie's reach. She flung herself at it, racket extended, but missed, stumbled, and fell flat on her face as the ball bounced harmlessly past her.

A ragged cheer rang out, mixed with groans from Cassie's supporters. Cassie picked herself up and dusted off the green granules that clung to her knees. Surprisingly, she didn't feel too upset. In fact, she was almost relieved. She'd done her best, and she'd lost. But she still felt she'd proved a point. Girls *could* compete with boys. Laughing, she went to the net, hand outstretched to meet T.J.

"Good game!" she cried as his hot, sweaty hand engulfed hers.

"Likewise," he said, laughing too, though there was a hint of pain in his eyes and he seemed to be favoring his wounded foot. "You're a pro, Cassie! I'll never be able to say it was an easy victory. There are too many witnesses!"

Arm in arm, they left the court, surrounded by a crowd of onlookers offering congratulations and condolences. Claudia hung back with her parents, disturbed by the fleeting expression of pain she'd seen on T.J.'s tanned face. *And Cassie didn't notice*, she thought. *She didn't notice at all!*

Chapter Nine

After the match Cassie began to feel a lot worse, and she was more than willing to go home, particularly since T.J. had left immediately in order to give his foot a rest. The twins spent most of the afternoon stretched out in the sun. Cassie dozed a lot of the time, leaving Claudia to her own thoughts. She was proud of her sister, and she'd enjoyed the match, but she couldn't help worrying about T.J. *Because I love him*, she thought. *We have absolutely nothing in common, but that doesn't matter.* Watching her sister and T.J. on the tennis court that morning had only emphasized the fact that they were perfectly suited for each other. Claudia felt lonely, left out, and, though she didn't like to admit it, jealous.

That evening after supper, Cassie felt the exhaustion of the match and the cold. She couldn't seem to keep her eyes open, and long before her usual bedtime, she stumbled up the stairs yawning. She was sure T.J. would call her the next day, maybe even ask her for a date, and she wanted to be completely rested, without so much as a sniffle left of that miserable cold. Claudia and her parents sat on the dock admiring the red-gold of the sinking sun behind the trees.

As Claudia gazed at the scene before her, she became aware of something on the lake heading toward the camp, a canoe with one passenger. Soon she recognized T.J., and her heart began to pound. *I should go get Cassie,* she thought, but she didn't.

"Hi," said T.J., smiling up at Claudia and her parents as he pulled the canoe alongside the dock. "Thought I'd just check in on my worthy opponent."

"Cassie's gone to bed," Mrs. Fletcher informed him. "Her cold has really knocked her out."

Claudia reluctantly got to her feet. "I'll tell her you're here," she offered, but T.J. shook his head.

"No, that's OK, let her rest. She deserves it,

after the way she almost slaughtered me this morning!"

"How's the foot?" asked Mr. Fletcher.

"Much better, thanks. I kept completely off it after the match, and now it hardly hurts at all."

A silence fell on the group, broken only by the chirping of the crickets and the plaintive calls of birds returning to their nests as the sunlight faded.

T.J. suddenly turned to Claudia. "Would you like to take a ride in the canoe with me?" he asked. "I was going to ask you both, but if Cassie's gone to bed . . ." His voice trailed off uncertainly.

"I—I'd love to," said Claudia softly. "It's such a beautiful evening." *You really ought to wake Cassie,* urged the voice of her conscience. *She'll never forgive you if you don't.*

"I thought maybe we'd go down by the meadow, where the deer feed at sunset. It's a really pretty sight," T.J. said.

"Go ahead, Claudia," said her mother, smiling.

T.J. steadied the canoe as Claudia stepped carefully into it and seated herself in the bow. She had made a conscious decision to ignore that nagging voice in her head. After all,

Cassie really did need her rest, didn't she? T.J. steered the canoe away from the dock. The setting sun turned the lake a brilliant crimson, and the slender craft cut silently through the rippling water.

The Fletchers' dock receded into the distance as T.J. paddled across the lake. Claudia felt as if she were in the middle of a dream, a delicious dream, with hardly any sound, nothing but the glowing water and sky, the trees along the banks a purple blur, the mountains beyond sinking into the shadows. T.J. didn't say a word, and Claudia felt no need to break the silence. She felt completely at peace, totally content.

Soon T.J. steered the canoe into the shallows at the end of the lake, where long, tall grass merged into a peaceful meadow. The figures of grazing deer were silhouetted against the trees. It was so beautiful, Claudia caught her breath. She felt as though she and T.J. were invisible, or as if they were some other species of animal that the deer recognized and accepted without being afraid.

T.J. moored the canoe to a half-sunken stake that protruded from the still water and carefully made his way to the bow, stepping out onto the springy turf. He reached out his hand to Claudia, and she took it without a word, mesmerized by the utter peace of the scene before her. Hand in hand, they walked toward the deer. The meadow seemed to Claudia an enchanted place where words would be meaningless, a place where time stood still.

Claudia turned her face to T.J. She was filled with a quiet sense of belonging and of love for the boy who stood beside her. Gently he put his arm around her and led her onward.

"I've always wondered if it was true," T.J. whispered, his breath tickling her ear. "I mean, what they say about two people who wear braces."

"What do they say?" Claudia whispered back.

"That if they kiss, their braces will lock together."

Claudia stifled a laugh, though her heart was beating so wildly that she was sure T.J. must hear it. Slowly T.J. bent his head toward hers, and their lips met in a kiss so sweet that Claudia could hardly bear it.

It was T.J. who finally broke the spell. "It's *not* true," he breathed. "I didn't think it was, but I wanted to make sure."

"Were you just testing?" Claudia managed to say, in spite of the lump in her throat.

"No. I've wanted to kiss you for a long time." T.J. smiled and kissed her again. It was absolutely nothing like Walter's kiss when he'd said goodbye to her a little over a week ago—or was it a lifetime ago? This was a kiss she'd never forget, a kiss that made her tingle right down to her toes.

As she clung to him, breathless and weak, she was dimly conscious of the deer moving slowly into the shelter of the trees, conscious of the shadows blending with the shadows of the branches. The sky was no longer rose but dusky lavender, laced with deep purple streaks of cloud.

"Maybe we ought to go back," she murmured.

"Maybe so," T.J. agreed softly, though he seemed unable to tear his eyes from hers.

After an endless, magic moment, they moved side by side back toward the canoe. To Claudia, it seemed as though her feet didn't really touch the ground.

When they were seated in the canoe again, Claudia turned to T.J. in the semidarkness. Her entire being wanted to cry out, "I love you!" but something held her back. Everything was too new and unexpected for her to express what she was feeling. So she sat in silence, content to be carried along by the soundless motion of the canoe. She even managed to ignore the realization that ahead of them lay the real world—and Cassie, who loved T.J., too.

"Claudia?" T.J.'s voice startled her. "I'm sorry if I came on too strong. It's just that, well, like I said, I've wanted to kiss you almost since the first day we met. I've never felt this way before. I mean, I've had girlfriends, and I guess you've had boyfriends, too, but . . . you're special."

"No, I'm not," said Claudia, her voice soft, too. "There's nothing special about me at all. But I'm glad you think so. You're special, too," Claudia whispered almost too softly for T.J. to hear her.

Claudia realized that T.J. was hugging the far shore of the lake rather than heading directly back to her house, and she was glad. It made the trip a little longer, stretched their precious time alone. She wouldn't think about Cassie just yet. That was something she'd have to deal with later.

"I have to work tomorrow," T.J. continued, "but if you're not doing anything tomorrow night, I thought maybe we could do something together, just the two of us."

Claudia's heart soared, then plummeted like a stone as she thought of Cassie's reaction. "I'm—I'm not sure if Mom and Dad have anything planned," she stammered.

"Well, if they don't, would you like to go out with me?"

Claudia sighed. "I'd like it more than anything!" she admitted. Then she added reluctantly, "What about Cassie?"

"What about her? Oh, you mean maybe she and Don could double with us? I guess that would be OK. I know Don really likes Cassie, but I'd kind of like to be with just you for a change. You're not *Siamese* twins, after all!" he said, laughing.

"That's not exactly what I meant." Claudia was glad that the darkness hid her face from him. "I guess I thought you were interested in Cassie, not me."

There, it was out. She waited for a response from T.J., and when none came, she was surprised to see the prow of the canoe nosing up against a dock. A moment later, T.J. had moored it and was getting out, reaching a hand down to her. She took it and climbed out, mystified. They were in front of a deserted cabin.

"Where are we?" she asked, puzzled.

"About half a mile from your place. I wanted to kiss you again." With that, he put his arms around her, drawing her close to him, and their lips met again in an even longer, sweeter kiss.

"Oh, T.J.!" Claudia whispered, resting her head against his chest.

"I think I've made it pretty clear which Fletcher I'm interested in," he said huskily. "Why did you think I liked Cassie? I mean, I *do* like her, she's a great person. But I'm not in love with her."

Claudia stood stock still, and a shiver ran through her entire body. "Do you mean? . . ." she faltered.

"I mean I'm in love with *you*," said T.J.

Claudia couldn't believe it. T.J. loved her! *Her*, Claudia, the quiet one, not Cassie, the vivacious, pretty, popular sister! Her eyes brimming with tears, she looked up at T.J. His face was illuminated by the pale light of the moon. "Thank you, T.J.," she said, and felt a tear creep down her cheek.

"You're welcome," he said and laughed. "That's not what a girl's supposed to say when

a guy tells her he loves her. She's either supposed to tell him to get lost or that she feels the
same way about him." The sudden uncer-
tainty in his voice tore at Claudia's heart.

"Oh, T.J., please don't get lost! I *do* love
you!" she whispered, raising her face for one
more kiss.

He grinned down at her, stroking her hair.
"That's more like it! Thank *you*, Miss
Fletcher!" He glanced up at the sky. "Hey, I
guess I'd better be getting you back home. It's
getting late."

They got back into the canoe, and Claudia
picked up a paddle. They followed the shore-
line until the lights of the Fletchers' cabin
were immediately before them.

"I'll call you tomorrow, OK?" T.J. suggested.
"Will you be home around noon? And if you're
free, we'll make plans for the evening. Maybe
we could do something really elegant, like
have dinner at the Adirondack Inn. I want to
do something special with you."

"I'll be home, T.J.," Claudia said. "I'll be
waiting for your call." She scrambled onto the
dock, then watched the canoe as it moved
across the moonlit lake to the opposite shore.
She touched her lips with one trembling
hand. *You didn't dream it,* she told herself.

Thankful that Cassie would be sound asleep, she wandered up the wooden steps to the deck, more stars in her eyes than were twinkling in the entire sky.

"Did you have a nice time?" Mrs. Fletcher looked up from her needlepoint as Claudia entered the living room.

"Need you ask?" said Mr. Fletcher teasingly at the sight of Claudia's glowing face. "Never mind, Lydia, she's in another world." Smiling, he went back to his book.

Claudia barely heard her parents' words. T.J.'s image, his voice, the feel of his arms around her, the touch of his lips on hers were her only reality. She wandered up the stairs, her mind and heart filled with special memories.

"Where were you, for heaven's sake!" Cassie's voice broke through Claudia's reveries. Suddenly she felt confused and guilty, as though she'd committed a secret crime.

"Oh, hi, Cass," she said, trying to keep her voice normal as she came into the darkened room. Cassie was sitting up cross-legged on her bunk, wide awake.

"I just woke up. It's OK if you turn on the light. My nose is all clogged up. Hand me some tissues, will you?"

Silently Claudia pulled a handful of tissues from the box on the bureau and passed them up to her twin. She began getting undressed, avoiding Cassie's eyes.

"Where'd you go? I was dozing, and I heard voices. Was T.J. here?"

"Yes. Yes, he was." Claudia pulled her nightgown over her head. "I'm going to brush my teeth." Quickly she scooted for the bathroom, her thoughts in turmoil. How could she tell Cassie what had happened? How could she *not* tell her? They'd never kept secrets from each other. They'd always shared everything. *You're not Siamese twins*, T.J. had said. But Claudia realized that in a way, he was wrong. They weren't joined by any physical bond, but by thoughts and feelings. *I have to tell Cassie*, she thought, and her stomach curled into a tight ball of anxiety.

"What did you do, brush every tooth individually?" Cassie teased when at last Claudia came back to their room.

"I have to be careful because of the braces," Claudia replied. "You know that." She turned off the light.

"Sure."

Claudia lay in the dark, hoping Cassie would leave it at that, but the familiar "Night,

131

Claude" was not forthcoming. She was so tense and nervous that when Cassie finally spoke, she jumped as though she'd been shot.

"Claude?"

"What?"

"So if T.J. was here, what did he say? Did he ask for me? Why didn't you wake me up? How's his foot?"

Claudia decided to answer the last question first. "He said his foot's OK."

"Good." There was a long, awkward silence. "Why did he come? Why didn't you wake me?"

Claudia clutched her pillow to her chest. "He asked how you were feeling. Mom told him you were zonked from your cold. He said you deserved a rest after the way you almost beat him this morning."

"And then what?"

"Well, he wanted to take us out in the canoe to see the deer feed in the meadow at the end of the lake. . . ."

"I see." Long pause. "So you went with him?"

"Yes."

"And?"

"Cass, I'm really tired. I'll tell you in the morning."

"Tell me what?"

You have to say it, Claudia thought to herself. "Well, we—T.J. and I—T.J. said . . ."

"Claudia, tell me!"

Claudia sat up, the pillow still clutched in her arms like a shield. "We went to the meadow, and we looked at the deer. They're really beautiful, Cass. We'll have to go sometime so you can see them. They weren't afraid of us at all," she babbled.

"Claude, *what happened*?"

"He—he kissed me. He said he loves me."

She could hear Cassie breathing. There was no other sound except the ever-present lapping of tiny waves on the shore. Even the night birds seemed to have quieted down.

"You're kidding," Cassie said at last, her voice throaty and raw.

"No, I'm not, Cass. And I told him I love him too. Because I do. I honestly do!" Claudia's voice broke on the last words, and she buried her face in the pillow.

"I don't believe it!" Cassie sounded astonished. Claudia heard the bedsprings creak above her as her sister changed position. "He loves *you*." Cassie's voice in the darkness was flat, without expression, but Claudia could hear the hurt underneath the toneless words.

"I didn't *do* anything, Cass, really I didn't!"

133

Claudia whispered. "I know how you must feel, but I didn't try to steal him from you. I was so surprised I didn't know what to do. And I was so . . . happy. I shouldn't have been, because I know how you feel about him, but I couldn't help it. It just sort of happened."

"He's in love with *you*," Cassie murmured again, barely audibly. And all the time I thought . . ."

"I did too, Cass. I thought it was you he was interested in. Even though I wanted him to like me, I thought he didn't care about me at all. And when he told me he did . . ."

"Yeah. I understand." Cassie sneezed. "I think I'll go to sleep now. Congratulations."

"Cassie . . ."

"Night, Claude."

Chapter Ten

Neither Claudia nor Cassie slept very well that night. Both lay awake, tossing and turning, but neither spoke. Claudia alternated between absolute bliss at knowing how T.J. felt about her and guilt-ridden misery about how Cassie felt about T.J.

Cassie was plunged into deep gloom, punctuated by bursts of anger and jealousy that she could not suppress. The strength of her emotions unnerved her. How could she possibly feel so angry at her sister, her very own twin sister, her best friend? But on the other hand, how could she help but feel hurt, rejected, and desolate?

Cassie had a powerful imagination, and in her mind's eye she could imagine as clearly as though it were on a movie screen T.J. putting his arms around Claudia and kissing her. The picture filled her with such misery that she wanted to burst into tears. But she knew Claudia would hear, and so she buried her face in her pillow and willed herself not to cry. *She betrayed me,* she thought melodramatically. *My very own sister stole the man I love!* Deep down, Cassie knew that since T.J. had never been hers to begin with, it wasn't fair to say Claudia had stolen him. Still, the words pounded through her restless brain. *I'll never forgive her, never!* The fact that her unshed tears were clogging up her nose only made matters worse. *Maybe I'll get really sick,* she thought, wallowing in self-pity. *I'll get sicker and sicker, and when I'm finally dying, T.J. will realize how much I love him.*

She pictured herself pale and wan, lying on the couch downstairs, eyes bright with fever, a brave smile playing over her dry lips. She could see Claudia standing there, tears streaming down her cheeks, as T.J. fell to his knees beside her, pressing her wasted hand in his. "I didn't know how much you cared," he would say, trembling with emotion.

And she would reply in a faint whisper, "That's all right, T.J. I understand."

The first birdcalls of the morning were filling the air when Cassie finally fell into an exhausted sleep. Her last thought before she dozed off was that she'd have to write everything down in her diary. She'd do it first thing in the morning. . . .

Claudia awakened very early, feeling far from rested. She slipped out of her nightgown and pulled on her bathing suit. Maybe a quick dip in the lake would help her get her head together. She brushed her hair and braided it quickly into one plait, glancing over her shoulder from time to time to see if Cassie's eyes were open. She was very thankful to see that her sister was still sound asleep.

Claudia tiptoed down the stairs and out onto the deck, breathing in the fresh, clean morning air. She wondered if T.J. was awake. She strained her eyes, but she could see no sign of life on the Howards' dock. Holding on to the railing, she rapidly ran through her exercises, realizing from the way her muscles complained that she'd been neglecting her warm-ups lately, ever since T.J. had "spied" on her that first morning. *And I thought I didn't like him*, she mused, smiling faintly. The memory of his kisses sent delightful chills

137

up and down her spine. And then the thought of Cassie jerked her out of her daydream. *Does she hate me?* she wondered as she walked down the wooden steps to the dock. She couldn't. She mustn't.

Claudia dove into the water and swam vigorously for a few minutes, trying to escape from her disturbing thoughts. Then she climbed back onto the dock and dried herself on a dew-damp towel. She decided to take a walk in the woods; she had to figure out what to do about T.J., about Cassie, about everything.

But when Claudia returned half an hour later to find her parents and Cassie having breakfast on the deck, she was no closer to a solution than she'd been when she left. She sat down in her accustomed place next to Cassie, avoiding her sister's eyes. Though the ham and cheese omelet Mrs. Fletcher had made smelled delicious, neither Claudia nor Cassie was able to eat very much of it. Their parents carried the burden of the conversation until the twins' silence could no longer be ignored.

"What's the matter with you two?" Mr. Fletcher asked.

"Your cold isn't worse, is it, Cassie?" asked

their mother anxiously. "Your eyes and nose are so red."

Cassie shook her head. "No, I feel OK."

"What about you, Claudia? You're not coming down with Cassie's cold, are you?"

"No, Mom. I didn't sleep very well last night, that's all."

Claudia got up from her seat and began clearing the table. From force of habit, Cassie joined her. As they washed the dishes in the kitchen, Claudia suddenly turned to her twin and whispered, "I think we'd better talk."

Cassie raised her eyebrows. "What's there to talk about? You and T.J. are madly in love. Period. End of conversation." Cassie hated the way her voice sounded, harsh and angry, but there was nothing she could do about it. "I suppose he's asked you out on a real date, one on one, huh?"

Claudia felt her cheeks flaming. "Well, as a matter of fact . . ." She hadn't mentioned it before because she'd been trying to think of some way to bring the subject up without hurting Cassie further. "He's calling me today at noon. He wants to—to take me out tonight. But I won't go if it's going to make you miserable," she said unhappily.

Cassie shrugged, trying to look as if it didn't

139

matter to her. "Far be it from me to disturb your love life! As a matter of fact, Don said something yesterday after the match about him and me doubling with Pat and her boyfriend, Larry, tonight. I guess he knew T.J. would be occupied with you. He's going to call this afternoon. I'll probably go. I mean, *please* don't think I'm going to sit around and *mourn* just because you have a date, for goodness' sake!"

Cassie slammed the cabinet door viciously and left the kitchen without waiting for her sister's reaction.

She does hate me, thought Claudia dismally. *My very own sister hates me, and it's all my fault. I should have woken her up last night. She should have gone with us. Then none of this would have happened.* She tried to recapture the thrill of T.J.'s kisses and the excitement she'd felt in the tender circle of his arms, but she couldn't. Claudia felt more alone than ever before in her life.

But when the phone rang promptly at noon, Claudia dashed to answer it as though she had wings on her heels. Hearing T.J.'s voice made her feel much better, especially since Cassie was out of earshot. T.J. said he would pick Claudia up at six for dinner at the Adirondack Inn.

Shortly after that the phone rang again. This time it was Don for Cassie. Lingering on the deck, Claudia heard her sister agree to go out with him and Pat and Larry that night. Somehow that made things seem a little less awful. At least she wouldn't have to worry about Cassie moping around the cabin, brooding over Claudia's date with T.J. And Don was really fun, in spite of being clumsy. He was actually good-looking, too. And he obviously liked Cassie a lot. Maybe Cassie would decide that she liked him better than T.J., though Claudia couldn't imagine anyone doing that. *Oh, Cass, please be happy*, she prayed, and crossed her fingers the way she had when she was younger.

When it was finally time to dress for her date with T.J., Claudia gathered up her clothing and makeup kit and headed for the bathroom. Cassie was getting ready for her date with Don in their bedroom, but neither sister felt like exchanging confidences and giggles the way they usually did when they had dates.

The afternoon had seemed endless. Both Claudia and Cassie had tried to keep up a pretense of normal behavior for their parents' benefit, but Claudia was sure they hadn't been fooled for a minute. Claudia was eager to get away from the tension that had cast a pall over the entire day. She thought about T.J. and their special date at the Adirondack Inn. After all, it was a dream come true. Claudia didn't want anything to spoil the evening to come.

Claudia chose a white Indian cotton dress with a ruffled neckline. She decided to be daring and wear it off the shoulder. The dazzling white of the dress emphasized her tan, and she scooped her hair back from her face with a white headband. Leaning close to the tiny mirror over the sink, she carefully applied silvery green eyeshadow and apricot-colored lip gloss. She stood back, examining her reflection critically. "I look like a nurse," she said aloud, frowning at her all-white image in the mirror. She needed a spark of color to liven up her color scheme. Suddenly she remembered Cassie's coral necklace. It would be perfect! She was about to dash to their bedroom and ask if she could borrow it, when she remembered. No, she couldn't ask Cassie to lend her a necklace when she was going out with the boy Cassie loved.

Instead, she went back into the room and, not looking at Cassie, began to rummage through the jewelry she'd brought to Green Lake. She settled for a slender gold chain with a small golden C hanging from it, which she carried back to the bathroom. As she fastened it around her neck, she remembered that Cassie had one just like it. They'd received them as presents from their grandma and grandpa Fletcher on their sixteenth birthdays. Would Cassie be wearing hers that night? Claudia wondered. Well, what if she was? Cassie could wear whatever she liked. T.J. had been right when he'd said they weren't Siamese twins, after all.

Claudia took one last look in the mirror and decided she looked great. She was ready to go. Then she felt a moment of panic. What did she do now? She couldn't very well hide in the bathroom until T.J. came to pick her up, but the last thing in the world she wanted was to face Cassie.

A brisk knock on the bathroom door made her spin around.

"Claudia, are you ever coming out?" It was Cassie, sounding petulant and annoyed. "I need to brush my teeth, *if* you don't mind."

Claudia quickly opened the door. "Sure. I'm through. Come on in."

Cassie glanced at her as she passed. She was wearing white pants and a yellow knot top. And she *was* wearing her gold C necklace.

"You look great," said Cassie, reaching for her toothbrush.

"Thanks. So do you."

Claudia hesitated on the threshold, clutching her makeup case. "Have fun tonight," she said softly.

"You, too." Cassie bent over the basin, scrubbing her teeth vigorously.

Suddenly Claudia giggled. "With all that foam around your mouth, you look like a mad dog!"

"If you don't watch out, I'll bite you in the leg!" Cassie responded, grinning. For a moment it was just like old times. Then Cassie turned away abruptly. "Give T.J. my regards," she snapped, spitting into the basin and turning on the water full force.

"Right."

It's not like old times, Claudia thought miserably, going back to the bedroom. *Will it ever be the same again?*

* * *

"Didn't you like your dinner? You hardly ate anything at all." T.J. leaned anxiously across the candlelit table at the Adirondack Inn, trying to understand Claudia's troubled expression.

"No—I mean, yes—it was delicious. I'm not very hungry, I guess," Claudia stammered. "The food's really good, T.J., and the inn is terrific. I wish Cassie . . ." She broke off and toyed with her dessert. It didn't seem right, somehow, that Cassie wasn't there to share everything, the way she'd always been before. Claudia felt as though part of her were missing. She looked up and met T.J.'s eyes. She loved him so much—but she loved Cassie, too.

"Well, if you're finished, let's take a walk. There's a great lookout point about half a mile away. We could watch the sunset from there," T.J. suggested, reaching out and taking her hand.

Claudia's fingers tingled at his touch, and she smiled. "I'd like that," she said softly. She'd try to put Cassie out of her mind and just enjoy being with T.J. She didn't want to ruin what ought to be the best evening of her entire life.

But even after they left the sprawling old inn behind, she couldn't shake her feeling of guilt. And when T.J. gently placed his hands on her

145

shoulders and turned her to face him, Claudia was so torn by divided loyalties that her eyes filled with tears and she broke away, walking swiftly to the edge of the lookout point. It was wrong, all wrong!

"Claudia, what's the matter?" T.J. asked. He stepped close to her and put his arm around her shoulder. She wanted so much to throw her arms around him and tell him everything. But the thought of Cassie held her back, and she tore herself away, unable to speak.

T.J.'s arm fell to his side, and he looked down at her, perplexed. "Hey, I'm sorry for whatever it is I did. Because I must have done something, or you wouldn't be acting this way. Last night I thought you said . . . What's *with* you, Claudia?"

Claudia brushed a tear from her eye and drew a trembling breath. "I—I'm all mixed up!"

T.J. walked away, sat down on a rock, and picked at the moss growing there. When he finally spoke again, his voice was calm and steady, but she could tell he was very upset. "I never asked you if there was somebody else in your life, somebody back home. I guess I thought you would have told me. Is that it? Is there somebody else? If there is, I want to know."

Unable to look at him, Claudia wrapped her arms around herself, shivering in the sudden chill as the last rays of the sun disappeared. "There *is* somebody else," she heard herself say in a voice that sounded as if it belonged to another person. "And I should have told you. But I—I couldn't." Cassie's tight, withdrawn face appeared before her mind's eye.

"Somebody you love a lot?"

"Yes—somebody I love a lot."

The silence was overpowering. Claudia heard every birdcall, every cricket chirp, even the sound of the breeze whispering through the leaves of the trees above her.

"Well." T.J.'s face was hidden by the shadows of the overhanging trees. A forced, unnatural laugh reached Claudia's ears, and she cringed. "I should have asked. Now I know."

"Now you know," Claudia echoed miserably.

"I guess we ought to be heading back home," T.J. said, standing up. "I should have realized that a girl like you would have a boyfriend. I just wish you'd told me sooner." He started down the path back to the inn and the parking lot. Claudia felt as though her heart were breaking into tiny fragments in her chest.

The ride home was totally silent. Claudia sat pressed up against the door, as far away from T.J. as she could manage. When they reached the cabin, she bolted for the safety of her room after a brief good night. Cassie had not yet returned from her date with Don, and her parents had apparently gone out. Claudia fell onto her bunk, and at last the tears that she had tried to blink back for the past half hour flowed freely, soaking her pillow. She'd done it. T.J. would never ask her out again. What more could Cassie want?

"Did you both have good times last night?" asked Mr. Fletcher the next morning at breakfast. "I have to hand it to T.J., he certainly got you home nice and early, Claudia. Your mother and I came home from the movies about ten, and you were already in bed."

"It was fine, and yes, I got in early," Claudia said quietly.

"I got home about eleven, I guess," said Cassie. "We went roller-skating, can you believe it? I haven't been roller-skating since I was about ten." She giggled. "Then we went to some pizza place where the kids hang out. If I

148

burned up any calories skating, I put them all back on. We all ought to go to the skating rink sometime. It was really fun."

Claudia sat silently beside her sister. Her hair, still damp from her swim, hung loosely around her shoulders and partially concealed her solemn expression. She didn't look like a girl who'd just had her first date with a boy she was nuts about.

Had T.J. kissed her again? Cassie wondered, glancing sideways at her. She felt a twinge of jealousy, but it was only a twinge, not the raging torment she'd felt when she had first learned that T.J. preferred Claudia to her. "What about you, Claude? How was the Adirondack Inn?" she asked.

Claudia looked up, and Cassie saw that her eyes were puffy, as though she'd been crying. Something must have happened last night, she thought. But what?

"It was fine," Claudia replied.

Claudia sounded like a broken record, thought Cassie impatiently. "Did you go anywhere after dinner?" she asked.

"No, just home."

Mrs. Fletcher looked closely at Claudia, puzzled by her daughter's lack of enthusiasm.

She caught Cassie's eye, her expression saying *Something's definitely wrong.*

"I think I'll go for a walk," said Claudia suddenly, standing up. "I saw some blackberries in the woods this morning. I'll take a basket and see if I can find them again."

"I'll go with you," said Cassie. Whatever it was that was making her sister unhappy, she was determined to find out. Then, remembering her sharpness with Claudia the night before, she added hesitantly, "If you don't mind, that is."

Claudia shrugged. "Sure. See you later, Mom, Dad."

A few minutes later, Claudia and Cassie were walking in uncomfortable silence through the trees on the other side of the road that separated their cabin from the forest. Sunlight filtered through the branches overhead, and low bushes caught at the girls' ankles as they followed the narrow path.

"This is probably a deer track, don't you think, Claude?"

"Probably," said Claudia.

Cassie couldn't stand it any longer. "What's the matter?" she asked anxiously. "Didn't you have a good time last night?"

For a moment she thought Claudia wasn't

going to respond, and then she noticed a single tear trickling down her sister's cheek. "Claude, what *is* it? Please tell me!"

Claudia flipped her hair back over one shoulder with her hand. Drawing a trembling breath, she turned to face Cassie and said, "It was a mistake. The whole thing was a big mistake. I won't be seeing T.J. anymore. He's all yours, Cass."

Cassie was thunderstruck. "What are you talking about? Did you have an argument or something? What gives?"

Claudia shook her head and walked on, oblivious to the brambles that scratched her legs. "No, we didn't argue. It's just that . . . he asked me . . . I told him . . ." Her voice choked up, and she plunged ahead, the empty basket swinging from her hand.

"What did you tell him? Come on, Claude! We've always told each other everything. What happened?"

"There's the blackberry patch," said Claudia, making for a clump of bushes among the trees. "Start picking!"

"Claudia Fletcher, you are driving me *crazy!*" snapped Cassie, her patience almost at an end. Following her twin, she seized Claudia's arm and spun her around so they

151

were face to face. "Forget the blackberries! I want to know what's wrong!"

Claudia wrenched her arm away and began flinging berries into the basket. Cassie could hardly hear her words. She seemed almost to be talking to herself. "The Adirondack Inn is beautiful. The food was delicious. But afterward, when T.J. wanted to—when he—" She whirled around, dropping the basket on the ground. "I couldn't stop thinking about how you feel about him, and it wasn't right. It just wasn't right! So when he asked me if there was somebody else, somebody I hadn't told him about, I said there was. Someone I cared about very much, someone I couldn't bear to hurt. He thought I was talking about another boy. I didn't tell him it was . . ."

"Me," supplied Cassie numbly. "You did that for *me*?"

Claudia picked up the basket and began picking berries so that she wouldn't have to look at Cassie. "You're my sister. When I had to decide between the two of you, I chose you."

Cassie felt as if someone had hit her hard. She stood staring at her twin in amazement. "You chose me," she repeated softly, and suddenly she felt about two feet tall, the smallest, meanest person in the world. "Oh, Claude, you're a real nut-job, you know?" She could hardly get the words out because of the tears that threatened to choke her. Suddenly she turned and began running back down the path toward the cabin.

"Cass, Cass, where are you going?" Claudia called after her.

Cassie didn't answer. She just kept running until she reached the cabin. When she got there, she dashed for the phone. Then she realized she didn't know the number of the Green Lake store. Frantically she riffled through the pages of the phone book, found the listing and dialed the number. When somebody answered, she said breathlessly, "I want to speak to T.J. Howard. It's important!"

Chapter Eleven

Claudia returned about an hour later, her basket filled with berries, and her heart filled with misery. She knew she ought to be feeling virtuous and content since she'd cleared the field for Cassie and T.J., but instead she felt worse than ever. Now she knew the true meaning of the old saying "Virtue is its own reward." It meant that you wouldn't get any *other* reward. She felt empty and dead inside. She certainly hadn't expected Cassie to react the way she had, running off like that with hardly a word. *They're probably together this very minute*, she thought. *Cassie obviously couldn't wait to see him. Well, I can hardly blame her. She's in love with him. Of course she wanted to see him immediately. Well, I wanted her to be happy, and I guess she is.*

Mrs. Fletcher was delighted with the berries and promised to make a blackberry cobbler for dessert that night. "We thought we'd go to that funny little museum in Andersville this afternoon," she said brightly. "Unless you and T.J. have other plans."

"No, we don't have any plans at all," said Claudia. "Where's Cass?" she asked, though she was sure she knew.

"She made a phone call and went off somewhere in a terrific rush," said Mrs. Fletcher, giving her daughter a searching look. "Claudia, what's the problem between you two? You're both acting very strangely."

"No problem," replied Claudia dully. "Everything's fine, Mom."

"I hate to say this, honey, but I don't believe you. Want to tell me about it?"

Claudia hesitated, then shook her head. "No, there's nothing to say. Nothing at all."

She was conscious of her mother's concerned gaze following her as she left the kitchen and plodded up the stairs to her bedroom. *It had to happen sooner or later. We were bound to fall in love with the same guy. I guess I can't compete with Cassie. T.J. will find out that he loves her, not me. He's probably realizing that right now. . . .*

*　　*　　*

"Listen, T.J., I wouldn't have asked you to meet me like this if it wasn't an emergency."

T.J. looked at Cassie sitting beside him on the stony beach and locked his arms around his knees, his lunch bag beside him. For the first time in his life, he had no appetite.

"What's up?" he asked, trying to make it sound as though he was interested in what Cassie was about to say.

"*Everything!*" cried Cassie urgently. "Claudia doesn't know I'm here. She'd kill me if she knew what I'm going to tell you."

T.J. picked up a small flat stone and skipped it across the water. It leaped three times, then sank, leaving widening circles on the lake. He stared at the ripples, but all he saw was Claudia's face. He wished Cassie would go away and leave him alone to brood.

But she didn't. Instead she leaned closer to him, her face eager and intense. She seemed about to burst forth with some incredible revelation, then sank back. "I don't quite know how to say this," she faltered. "It's kind of embarrassing."

T.J. sighed. "If you're going to tell me that Claudia has a boyfriend back home, I already know. She told me last night." His voice was expressionless as he poked at the pebbles between his feet.

"But she *doesn't*! That's what I have to tell you! There was a guy who liked her—we called him Wally the Wimp—but she didn't like him in the same way. Claudia does *not* have a boyfriend, believe me!"

T.J.'s warm brown eyes met Cassie's, and she saw confusion and hurt in them. "Then why did she tell me she did? Boy, she must really hate me to make up a story like that!"

"She didn't make up the story, *you* did!" cried Cassie, jumping to her feet. "She told you there was someone she loved and she didn't want to make that person unhappy. Well . . ." The next words stuck in her throat, and she fell silent.

"Yes?" T.J. was at a total loss. He had no idea what Cassie was trying to say.

"That person is *me*," Cassie finally blurted out, her face turning crimson.

"Hey, wait a minute. I don't know what you're talking about," said T.J., bewildered. "I think I missed something there."

"You sure did!" said Cassie, moving down to the water's edge. "Look, I don't know how to tell you this, but . . ."

"Cassie, spit it out!"

T.J. dashed over to her and grabbed her arm. "Hey, I don't know what's going on in your mind, but I *do* know that your sister turned me off last night but good. Now you tell me that she doesn't have a boyfriend at home and that the person she was talking about is you. What gives?"

Cassie would have liked to turn around and run as fast as she could away from T.J. and Claudia's problem. But she remembered what Claudia had done for her and steeled herself.

"Claudia told you there was somebody she cared about very much, somebody she didn't want to hurt, right?"

T.J. nodded.

"Well, she was talking about me. She thought that I had, well, kind of a crush on you. I don't know where she got that idea," she continued airily, "but she was afraid I'd be unhappy if she kept on going out with you. So she said what she said last night. She didn't want to hurt me, so she hurt you instead. And she's really miserable right now because she thinks *you* think what she meant you to think. Only what she meant you to think isn't true, see what I mean?"

T.J. stared at her, and then, slowly, a grin

broke over his face. "Claudia thought that you . . . I'll be darned!"

"That's what she thought," Cassie mumbled. "Silly, isn't it?"

"And there really isn't anybody else?" T.J. asked eagerly.

"Nobody," Cassie repeated. She scraped her toes against some pebbles.

T.J. flung his arms around her and gave her such a powerful hug that it almost knocked the breath out of her. "Hey, that's terrific!" he shouted. "Is she home now? Can I call her?"

"Feel free." Cassie sighed.

"Wow, girls are weird!" said T.J. "If Claudia had a brain in her head, she'd know that you and I are nothing but friends. But she *does* have a brain in her head. She's the brightest, most wonderful girl I've ever met! She's really special." He started off for the store, then turned and grabbed Cassie's hand. "Thanks for telling me, I really mean that. You're a pal, Cassie. Anytime you need a favor, just ask me!"

Cassie watched as T.J. sprinted up the beach. The brown bag containing his untouched lunch lay near her feet. On impulse, Cassie swung back her leg and kicked it as far out into the lake as she could.

159

Somehow, it made her feel a little better. She stared at the bag, floating like a small, fat boat. She hoped T.J. wasn't hungry.

Sighing, she turned away and began walking back to the road, picking up her discarded sandals on the way. As she walked along, the sun beating down on her head and shoulders, she wondered what T.J. would say to Claudia. Whatever it was, it was sure to make her sister ecstatically happy.

When she got back, she'd hear all about it, she was sure. And that night she'd write everything down in her diary. That always helped, somehow.

Claudia hung up the phone in a daze. She sank down into the nearest chair, hardly able to believe what had just happened. She'd almost dropped the receiver when she'd heard T.J.'s voice in her ear.

"Claudia? It's T.J. Are you doing anything tonight? Because if you're not, I'll pick you up right after work!"

"But, T.J., I told you—" Claudia began.

"I know what you told me, and I know *why* you told me. Cassie just filled me in. But it's OK. You were wrong, Claudia. Cassie doesn't care about me except as a friend, and that's the way I feel about her. So nobody's feelings are going to be hurt—except mine, if you won't meet me tonight."

"Oh," said Claudia in a small, weak voice. "What—what exactly did Cassie say?"

"Oh, just that you thought she liked me and that's why you let me believe you had a boyfriend back home. It was kind of confusing, but that's what it boiled down to. Claudia, I'll come by your place around five-thirty, OK? And, Claudia, I love you."

"I love you, too," murmured Claudia, almost too stunned to speak.

Now she sat staring into space, astonished. Cassie had actually pretended she didn't care about T.J. for her sake, just as she herself had given him up for Cassie. And T.J. had said he loved her again, just like that. He still loved her!

"Oh, poor Cass! *Dear* Cass," she said aloud.

Just then poor, dear Cass came into the cabin, the screen door slamming loudly behind her.

"Hi! Where are Mom and Dad? Get any interesting phone calls lately?" she asked, glancing mischievously at her sister. Claudia just stared at her, her eyes brimming with tears. "Oh, come on, Claude! You're not going to cry all over me, are you?"

"I don't know where Mom and Dad are," said Claudia, blinking away her tears. Then she leaped out of her chair and threw her arms around her sister. "Why did you do it? *How* could you do it? You're in love with him yourself!"

Cassie returned the hug, then shrugged out of her sister's embrace and walked over to the window. "I guess maybe I'm not as much in love with him as I thought I was," she confessed, frowning as she tried to sort out her emotions. "I think I'm kind of in love with him, but maybe that's because you are. We've always done everything together. I guess maybe I thought we had to share T.J., too. When I went out with Don last night, I actually had a very good time. I realized I must not really be in love with T.J. if I could forget about him so quickly. And when you told me this morning you'd given him up because of me, I knew I didn't love him enough for you to be so unhappy." She glanced over her shoulder at Claudia. "Does that make any sense?"

Claudia nodded slowly. "You don't still hate me?" she asked.

"Oh, Claude! I never hated you. How could

I? You're like part of me. Only you're *not* part of me, and that's what it's all about, I guess. We're twins, but we're separate people. Maybe it's time we got used to the idea."

Claudia joined her sister by the window, slipping her arm around Cassie's waist. "Do you remember that O. Henry story, 'The Gift of the Magi'?" she asked.

"Sure. That's the one where the guy pawns his gold watch to buy his wife a comb for her beautiful hair and *she* sells her hair to buy him a chain for his gold watch. I think I see what you mean," said Cassie, blinking back her own tears. "We both gave up what was most important for each other."

"Only I end up with a wonderful present, and you end up with—"

Cassie's giggle broke out in spite of herself. "I end up with Don!"

Claudia couldn't help laughing, too. "Don's not so bad. How do you feel about him?" she asked eagerly. "You said you had a good time last night."

"Yeah, I did. So you see what I meant. If I'd really been in love with T.J., I'd probably have been miserable the whole time. Don't get me wrong, I'm definitely *not* in love with Don, no way! He's a great guy, and I like him a lot, but I don't feel about him the way you do about T.J." Cassie leaned her head on Claudia's shoulder for a minute. "I wish I did. I wish we could both be in love at the same time—with different people."

"Maybe we will, someday," said Claudia softly. She felt peaceful and relaxed for the first time in days. "T.J.'s coming over after work tonight," she confided shyly. "Would you like to call Don? Maybe you two could double with us. I know T.J. wouldn't mind, and I'd love it!"

Cassie shook her head. "I don't think I'm up to that, not yet. Besides, I plan on making a very long entry in my diary tonight. I bet our grandchildren will really get a kick out of reading about how we both fell in love with the same boy. Kids never realize that their grandparents were young once."

Claudia groaned. "Can you imagine reading about a great romance in Grandma Fletcher's past?"

"Not to mention Grandmother Harbach. I bet she never so much as held hands with a boy before she got engaged to Granddad."

"But that's probably just what our grandchildren will think about us!" cried Claudia. "Will you let me read what you write?"

Cassie hesitated, then said, "Sure. After all, you're the co-star in this story."

In a few hours, I'll be seeing T.J., Claudia thought. *And once we go back home, it won't be long until he's at college. Then we'll see each other a lot. And Cassie will see Don, too. Maybe she'll fall in love with him. Or maybe she'll fall in love with somebody else real soon.*

It must be wonderful to be really in love, thought Cassie. *I guess I'll find out someday. And in the meantime I have Don. . . .*

The sisters grinned at each other. They were back on the same wavelength at last.

You'll fall in love with all the Sweet Dream romances. Reading these stories, you'll be reminded of yourself or of someone you know. There's Jennie, the *California Girl*, who becomes an outsider when her family moves to Texas. And Cindy, the *Little Sister*, who's afraid that Christine, the oldest in the family, will steal her new boyfriend. Don't miss any of the Sweet Dreams romances.

☐	24327	**SECRET IDENTITY #22** Joanna Campbell	$2.25
☐	24407	**FALLING IN LOVE AGAIN #23** Barbara Conklin	$2.25
☐	24329	**THE TROUBLE WITH CHARLIE #24** Jaye Ellen	$2.25
☐	22543	**HER SECRET SELF #25** Rhondi Villot	$1.95
☐	24292	**IT MUST BE MAGIC #26** Marian Woodruff	$2.25
☐	22681	**TOO YOUNG FOR LOVE #27** Gailanne Maravel	$1.95
☐	23053	**TRUSTING HEARTS #28** Jocelyn Saal	$1.95
☐	24312	**NEVER LOVE A COWBOY #29** Jesse Dukore	$2.25
☐	24293	**LITTLE WHITE LIES #30** Lois I. Fisher	$2.25
☐	23189	**TOO CLOSE FOR COMFORT #31** Debra Spector	$1.95
☐	23190	**DAYDREAMER #32** Janet Quin-Harkin	$1.95
☐	23283	**DEAR AMANDA #33** Rosemary Vernon	$1.95
☐	23287	**COUNTRY GIRL #34** Melinda Pollowitz	$1.95
☐	23338	**FORBIDDEN LOVE #35** Marian Woodruff	$1.95
☐	23339	**SUMMER DREAMS #36** Barbara Conklin	$1.95
☐	23340	**PORTRAIT OF LOVE #37** Jeanette Noble	$1.95
☐	23341	**RUNNING MATES #38** Jocelyn Saal	$1.95
☐	23509	**FIRST LOVE #39** Debra Spector	$1.95
☐	24315	**SECRETS #40** Anna Aaron	$2.25
☐	23531	**THE TRUTH ABOUT ME AND BOBBY V. #41** Janetta Johns	$1.95
☐	23532	**THE PERFECT MATCH #42** Marian Woodruff	$1.95

Prices and availability subject to change without notice.

Coming Soon . . .

Watch for the
SWEET VALLEY HIGH/SOAP OPERA
CELEBRATION CONTEST

Here's your chance to win an exciting all-expense-paid trip to New York City for three.

If you're one of the lucky winners . . .*

> You will take in the fabulous sights of New York, see a Broadway show, and visit a top beauty salon for a complete makeover!

> You will spend time on the set of a major soap opera and dine with a soap star!

> You will meet the creator of Sweet Valley High, Francine Pascal, in the elegant surroundings of one of the finest restaurants New York City can offer!

Watch for complete contest details at your local bookseller starting August, 1984!

*There will be two winners—one from the United States and one from Canada. The contest will apply only to Canada, the Continental U.S., Alaska and Hawaii.

☐ 23604 **Sweet Dreams: How To Talk Boys & Other Important People** $1.95
Catherine Winters

☐ 23375 **The Sweet Dreams Beautiful Hair Book** $1.95
Courtney DeWitt

☐ 23376 **The Sweet Dreams Body Book** $1.95
Julie Davis

☐ 23293 **The Sweet Dreams Fashion Book** $1.95
Patricia Bozic

☐ 23288 **The Sweet Dreams Love Book: Understanding Your Feelings** $1.95
D. Laiken & A. Schneider

Prices and availability subject to change without notice.

Buy them at your local bookstore or use this handy coupon for ordering:

☐	23969	**DOUBLE LOVE #1** Francine Pascal	**$2.25**
☐	23971	**SECRETS #2** Francine Pascal	**$2.25**
☐	23972	**PLAYING WITH FIRE #3** Francine Pascal	**$2.25**
☐	23730	**POWER PLAY #4** Francine Pascal	**$2.25**
☐	23943	**ALL NIGHT LONG #5** Francine Pascal	**$2.25**
☐	23938	**DANGEROUS LOVE #6** Francine Pascal	**$2.25**
☐	24001	**DEAR SISTER #7** Francine Pascal	**$2.25**
☐	24045	**HEARTBREAKER #8** Francine Pascal	**$2.25**
☐	24131	**LOVE ON THE RUN #9** Francine Pascal	**$2.25**

<u>Prices and availability subject to change without notice.</u>

Buy them at your local bookstore or use this handy coupon for ordering: